BUDDHIST TALES
for
YOUNG and OLD

Volume 1

Stories of the Enlightenment Being
Jātakas 1–50

BUDDHIST TALES
for YOUNG and OLD

Volume 1

Stories of the Enlightenment Being
Jātakas 1–50

Interpreted by
KURUNEGODA PIYATISSA MAHA THERA

Stories Told by
Todd Anderson

Illustrated by
Sally Bienemann, Millie Byrum, Mark Gilson

2nd Edition, Revised and Enlarged by
Kurunegoda Piyatissa Maha Thera and
Stephan Hillyer Levitt

Buddhist Tales for Young and Old

Volume 1: STORIES OF THE ENLIGHTENMENT BEING, Jātakas 1–50.
Interpreted by Kurunegoda Piyatissa Maha Thera. Stories Told by Todd Anderson. Illustrated by Sally Bienemann, Millie Byrum, Mark Gilson. 2nd edition, revised and enlarged by Kurunegoda Piyatissa Maha Thera and Stephan Hillyer Levitt. Parkside Hills, New York: Buddhist Literature Society, Inc., 2013. (1st edition, under the title PRINCE GOODSPEAKER, STORIES 1–50, 1995.)

Volume 2: STORIES OF THE ENLIGHTENMENT BEING, Jātakas 51–100, 514.
Interpreted by Kurunegoda Piyatissa Maha Thera. Stories Told by Todd Anderson. Illustrated by John Patterson. 2nd edition, revised and enlarged by Kurunegoda Piyatissa Maha Thera and Stephan Hillyer Levitt. Parkside Hills, New York: Buddhist Literature Society, Inc., 2013. (1st edition, under the title KING FRUITFUL, STORIES 51–100, 1996. 2nd ptg. of the 1st edition, together with KING SIX TUSKER AND THE QUEEN WHO HATED HIM, CHADDANTA-JATAKA (NO. 514) appended, [2004].)

Volume 3: STORIES OF THE ENLIGHTENMENT BEING, Jātakas 101–150.
Interpreted by Kurunegoda Piyatissa Maha Thera. Stories Retold by Stephan Hillyer Levitt. Parkside Hills, New York: Buddhist Literature Society, Inc., 2007.

Volume 4: STORIES OF THE ENLIGHTENMENT BEING, Jātakas 151–200.
Interpreted by Kurunegoda Piyatissa Maha Thera. Stories Retold by Stephan Hillyer Levitt. Parkside Hills, New York: Buddhist Literature Society, Inc., 2009.

Volume 5: STORIES OF THE ENLIGHTENMENT BEING, Jātakas 201–250.
Interpreted by Kurunegoda Piyatissa Maha Thera. Stories Retold by Stephan Hillyer Levitt. Parkside Hills, New York: Buddhist Literature Society, Inc., 2012.

Pariyatti Press
an imprint of
Pariyatti Publishing
www.pariyatti.org

First Pariyatti Edition, 2024
Published with the consent of Buddhist Literature Society, Inc.

ISBN: 978-1-68172-657-1 (Print)
ISBN: 978-1-68172-675-5 (PDF)
ISBN: 978-1-68172-676-2 (ePub)
ISBN: 978-1-68172-677-9 (Mobi)
Library of Congress Control Number: 2024936371

Cover illustration by Sally Bienemann, assisted by Arlene Yellen and cover design by Nalin Ariyarathne.

Foreword to the 2nd Edition

This 2nd edition of vols. 1 and 2 of *Buddhist Tales for Young and Old* was undertaken so as to bring the format of these volumes in line with that adopted in vols. 3–5.

These Jātaka stories as they have been handed down to us are accompanied in Buddhaghosa's text with "stories of the present" which narrate the circumstances under which the Buddha is reputed to have told the various fables and parables, and which grew up around these stories in the course of their transmission.

It is apparent that the "stories of the present" are integral to at least some of the stories in that some of the stories take their titles from these. Thus, for instance, the *Losaka-Jātaka* (No. 41), the two *Sāketa-Jātaka*-s (Nos. 68 and 237), the *Telapatta-Jātaka* (No. 96), the *Samiddhi-Jātaka* (No. 167), the *Kāmanīta-Jātaka* (No. 228), and the *Palāsa-Jātaka* and *Dutiya-Palāsa-Jātaka* (Nos. 229 and 230). In several instances, the main characters in the fables and parables take their names from the person in the "story of the present" about whom the story is told. So, for instance, in the *Rohiṇī-Jātaka* about a servant girl of the millionaire Anāthapiṇḍika named Rohiṇī (No. 45), and in the *Kālakaṇṇi-Jātaka* (No. 83) about a friend of Anāthapiṇḍika's named Kālakaṇṇi.

The fables and parables themselves, of course, in at least many instances pre-date the Buddha and at times can be found elsewhere in South Asian literature, as well.

Buddhaghosa's text also includes the "connection" between the "stories of the present" and the fables and parables – referred to as "stories of the past," which "connection" identifies the characters in the "stories of the present" with those in the "stories of the past" – the fables and parables as told here by Todd Anderson. The "connection" appears at the end of each Jātaka tale.

In vols. 3–5 we related the "stories of the present" and "connections" along with the Jātakas proper. We have here added them to the stories in vols. 1 and 2.

In vols. 3–5, we generally followed closely the late 13th c. – early 14th c. C.E. Sinhalese translation of the Jātaka stories by Virasiṁha Pratirāja for both the "stories of the present" and the "stories of the past," and for the "connections." In vols. 1 and 2, though, with the exception of the narration of the *Chaddanta-Jātaka* (No. 514) that was appended to vol. 2, the stories were more abbreviated. We have therefore in the main followed this practice here as well for this 2nd edition of vols. 1 and 2, abbreviating the "stories of the present" and the "connections."

On the whole, we have not altered here the text as told by Todd Anderson except for a few stylistic revisions here and there, and except that in a few places, mostly in vol. 2, additions and changes were necessitated on account of the addition of the "stories of the present" and the "connections." Also in a few places in vol. 2, changes had to be made in the specifics of a repeated story or in the specifics of two stories the telling of which had been here combined.

We have as well added here the Pāli titles of the various Jātaka stories for more ready recognition of the different stories. We have also added the Pāli names of the various characters the names of which were characterized in English by Todd Anderson earlier – giving these the first time the name is mentioned only; and for the purpose of clarity, in brackets, we have added various Pāli technical terms which terms were earlier characterized here in English only. When Pāli names were given in the translation earlier, we have added the appropriate diacritics. And we have added in footnotes points of general interest.

Further, for the sake of uniformity with vols. 3–5, we have here changed the way in which vols. 1 and 2 were titled.

The Pāli story titles, which Radhika Abeysekera, currently of Winnipeg, Manitoba, Canada, had also earlier suggested be added, very often focus on different points in, or aspects of the stories than the

English titles given to characterize the stories in vols. 1 and 2. On account of layout, an English rendering of these Pāli titles could not be given in place. We give here an English rendering of these titles for the stories in vol. 1:

1. *Apaṇṇaka-Jātaka* – A Story of Encouragement
2. *Vaṇṇupatha-Jātaka* – The Story of a Sandy Road
3. *Serivāṇija-Jātaka* – The Story of a Vendor from Seri
4. *Cullakaseṭṭhi-Jātaka (Cullaseṭṭhi-Jātaka)* – The Story of Cullakaseṭṭhi (or, Cullaseṭṭhi; The Younger Millionaire)
5. *Taṇḍulanāḷi-Jātaka* – The Story of a Measure of Dry Rice
6. *Devadhamma-Jātaka* – The Story of the Teaching of the Gods
7. *Kaṭṭhahāri-Jātaka* – The Story of One Who Collects Firewood
8. *Gāmaṇi-Jātaka* – The Story of (Prince) Gāmaṇi (Village Headman)
9. *Makhādeva-Jātaka* – The Story of (King) Makhādeva
10. *Sukhavihāri-Jātaka* – The Story of Dwelling in Happiness
11. *Lakkhaṇa-Jātaka (Lakkhaṇamiga-Jātaka)* – The Story of Lakkhaṇa (Beauty) / The Story of a Deer Named Lakkhaṇa
12. *Nigrodhamiga-Jātaka (Nigrodha-Jātaka)* – The Story of a Deer Named Nigrodha (Banyan) / The Story of Nigrodha
13. *Kaṇḍina-Jātaka* – The Story of Infatuation in the Course of Life's Impermanence
14. *Vātamiga-Jātaka* – The Story of a Deer Who Could Run as Fast as the Wind
15. *Kharādiya-Jātaka* – The Story of Rough Character[1]
16. *Tipallatthamiga-Jātaka (Sikkhākāma-Jātaka)* – The Story of a Skillful Deer[2] / The Story of One With a Desire to Learn
17. *Māluta-Jātaka* – The Story of the Wind
18. *Matakabhatta-Jātaka* – The Story of the Feast for Dead Ancestors
19. *Āyācitabhatta-Jātaka (Pāṇavadha-Jātaka)* – The Story of Promised Sacrifices / The Story About the Slaughter of Life
20. *Naḷapāna-Jātaka* – The Story of Sipping Through a Cane Straw

---

1   *kharādiya* – literally, 'rough, and so forth.'
2   *tipallattha* – literally, 'turning in three ways'; that is, 'skillful in all ways.'

---

3   *ājānīya* - such a horse knows what its rider wants it to do intuitively. So, also, *ājañña*, in Jātaka No. 24.

48. *Vedabbha-Jātaka* – The Story of a Magic Spell

49. *Nakkhatta-Jātaka* – The Story of an Auspicious Time

50. *Dummedha-Jātaka* – The Story of Unwise Actions

The transliteration system used for Pāli words and names is that of the U.S. Library of Congress Cataloging Service for Sanskrit and Prakrit languages in *Devanāgarī* script as in their Bulletin 64 (February 1964), with a few minor but standard variations. That for Sinhalese words and names, when these are given, is that of the U.S. Library of Congress Cataloging Service Bulletin 88 (January 1970). A guide to the pronunciation of Pāli words and names is given following this foreword.

We would like to thank Namal Kuruppu for preparing a JPEG file of the illustrations that accompany the stories in these vols. 1 and 2 so that they could be included here expeditiously. We would also like to thank the Ven. Sirisumana of the New York Buddhist Vihara for his instruction on incorporating the images in the text.

We hope our readers will receive this revised and enlarged edition of vols. 1 and 2 as well as they have received the earlier edition of vols. 1 and 2, and as well as they have received vols. 3–5.

Peace and health to all!

Kurunegoda Piyatissa Nayaka Maha Thero

Stephan Hillyer Levitt, Ph.D.

June, 2012

Buddhist Literature Society, Inc.

New York Buddhist Vihara

214-22 Spencer Avenue

Parkside Hills, New York 11427-1821, U. S. A.

A Guide to the Pronunciation of Pāli Words and Names

VOWELS

a	as *u* in but	u	as *u* in pull	ā	as *a* in father
ū	as *u* in rule	i	as *i* in pin	e	as *ay* in say
ī	as *i* in machine	o	as *o* in go		

CONSONANTS AND NASALS

k (guttural) like the English *k* in take or pick. kh as *kh* in lakehouse. g as *g* in pig. gh as *gh* in doghouse. The nasal ṅ is used with k, kh, g, and gh.

c (palatal) similar to *ch* in chalk, but unaspirated. ch as *ch* in chalk or church.

j like the English *g* in page. jh as *j* in joy, but even more aspirated. The nasal ñ as in Spanish Español is used with c, ch, j, and jh.

ṭ a retroflex sound, pronounced with the tongue curled back so that it touches the roof of the mouth. ṭh is the same sound, but aspirated. ḍ and ḍh are the voiced counterparts of these sounds. ṇ is the retroflex nasal. The difference between these sounds and the dentals, without dots, is not important for the general reader.

t (dental) similar to *t* in French or Italian. th as *th* in anthill. d similar to *d* in pod or paid. dh as *dh* in roundhouse. The nasal n is used with t, th, d, and dh.

p (labial) as *p* in English up. ph as *ph* in uphill. b as *b* in rub. bh as *bh* in clubhouse. The nasal m is used with p, ph, b, and bh.

ṁ as *ng* in sing. This is a nasal sound that lacks the closure of the organs required for the other nasal sounds.

SEMIVOWELS

y, r, l, v similar to their English counterparts. ḷ is a retroflex variant of l.

SIBILANT

s as *s* in saint or hiss.

ASPIRATE

h as *h* in hit.

Contents

1st Edition
Acknowledgements

The main computer system was generously provided by Thanh Van Nguyen, who also gave valuable technical assistance.

Ananda Ranasinghe was the word processing expert and teacher. He entered most of the text into the computer.

The storyteller's computer system was contributed by Karen Fazio, in memory of Beverly Vanice.

Illustrations

The illustrations on the frontispiece, pages 1, 4, 5, 8, 10, 15, 21, 28, 33, 39, 42, 45, 48, 56, 58, 60, 65, 75, 76, 85, 88, 94, 103, 106, 108, 114, 119, 135, 139, 142, 145, 147, 150, 155, 159, 164, 184, 186, 192 and 205 are by Sally Bienemann, assisted by Arlene Yellen. They are dedicated to Frank Campbell.

The illustrations on pages 127, 129, 132, 166 and 200 are by Millie Byrum.

The illustrations on pages 68, 72, 81, 98, 120, 180, 190 and 195 are by Mark Gilson.

Interpreter's Introduction to the 1ˢᵗ Edition

It is a pleasure to rewrite the Jataka stories in modern English understandable by western readers. To achieve this goal, the stories are being retold in order to convey the spirit and meaning. They are not scholarly word-for-word translations as have been done by others. The Pali Text Society has published the whole text in English translations done a hundred years ago. In Sri Lanka they were translated into Sinhalese in the 14th century, where they were known as *Pansiya Panas Jataka*.

In all Buddhist countries the Jataka tales were the major sources for developing the character of the people. They were used widely in preaching by monks and lay preachers. King Dutugemunu (2nd century B.C.), in Anuradhapura, paid for the support of preachers to teach Dhamma, the teachings of the Buddha. They usually used these stories in their sermons. Even the Venerable Arahant Maha Mahinda, who introduced Dhamma into Sri Lanka, used these stories to illustrate the truth of the teachings. Some were even used by the Lord Buddha in his teachings, and from him his followers learned them and passed them into popular use in society. Even earlier, the same types of stories were present in Vedic literature.

Greek myths, as well as the fables of Aesop, inherited them from the Vedas and Buddhism; Persia also took them from India. They later migrated into the stories of Chaucer in England and Boccaccio in Italy. The stories were used for a variety of purposes. In Sanskrit, the *Pancatantra* used them to teach Law and Economics, and the *Katha Sarit Sagara* used them for the development of knowledge, as well as just for enjoyment. In the past, people have been satisfied and fulfilled in many ways by hearing them in forms ranging from lessons to fairy tales.

By reading these stories, children and adults can develop their knowledge and learn how to face the difficult experiences of modern life. They can easily develop human values and good qualities like patience, forbearance, tolerance and the four sublime states of mind – loving-kindness, compassion, sympathetic joy and equanimity. The major purpose of these stories is to develop the moral and ethical values of the readers. Without them, people cannot be peaceful and happy in their hearts and minds. And the reader will find that these values are very different from those of the wider, violently acquisitive, ego-based society.

In this interpretation, changes are being made to the style of the old Jataka stories, and explanations are added, as is appropriate for children in the modern world. The lovely art work is also sometimes in a modern setting, to attract young and old to the truths contained in the tales.

The sources used have been as follows:

1. *Jataka Pali* (Colombo: Buddha Jayanti Tripitaka Series Publication Board, 1983) – original Pali stanzas.
2. *Jataka Pali* (Colombo: Simon Hewavitarane Bequest, 1926) – original Pali Jataka stories in Sinhalese characters.
3. *Sinhala Jataka Pot Vahanse* (Colombo: Jinalankara Press, 1928) – Sinhalese translation of Pali Jataka stories.
4. *Sinhala Jataka Pot Vahanse*, (Colombo: Ratnakara Bookshop, 1961) – Sinhalese translation of Pali Jataka stories.
5. *Jataka Pota*, ed. Lionel Lokuliyana (Colombo: M. D. Gunasena & Co., 1960) – Sinhalese translation of first fifty Pali Jataka stories.
6. *The Jataka or Stories of the Buddha's Former Lives*, ed. E. B. Cowell (London: Pali Text Society, 1981), 6 vols., index – English translation of Pali Jataka stories.
7. *Pansiyapanas Jataka Pot Vahanse* (Bandaragama: H. W. N. Prematilaka, 1987) – Sinhalese summaries of Pali Jataka stories.

In addition, "From the Storyteller to the Listeners" (below), contains a paraphrase taken from "Discourse With Canki", *Middle Length Sayings* (*Majjhima-Nikaya*), trans. I. B. Horner (London: Pali Text Society, 1975), II, 95, pp. 362-3. The title of the fourth story, "The Mouse Merchant", was originally in Somadeva, *The Ocean of Story (Katha Sarit Sagara)*, trans. C. H. Tawney (London: C. J. Sawyer, 1924).

The sequence numbers used for the stories are in the same order as in the *Jataka Pali* and *The Jataka or Stories of the Buddha's Former Lives* (above). Multiple sequence numbers indicate that identical, similar or partial stories are told in one version. The most complex example is "The Curse of Mittavinda", which requires explanation. Here the *Losaka* (41), the three *Mittavinda* (82, 104, 369) and the *Catu-Dvara* (439) *Jatakas* are combined. This is because the stanzas of 82, 104 and 369 all refer directly to the palaces described in 41 and 439, as well as to the wheel of torture described in 439. The latter retells the four palaces portion of 41, and then leads directly into the wheel of torture (*Ussada* hell) portion. To allow continuity, the ending of the wheel of torture portion is taken from 369, since in it Mittavinda does not die.

Since the stories include legends which are not actually canonical, the character traditionally said to be the Bodhisatta (the Buddha in a past life) is not necessarily identified in each rewritten story. A complete list is given separately in Appendix A for reference.

Many of the stories indicate several morals. Only one per story was selected for emphasis. Appendix B arranges these morals according to the three 'roots of unwholesomeness' (*akusala mulani*) paired with the opposing wholesome qualities, as follows:

1. Greed (*lobha*) – generosity (*dana*).
2. Anger (*dosa*) – loving-kindness (*metta*).
3. Delusion (*moha*) – wisdom (*panna*).

Appendix B can serve as an alternate sequence for reading the stories.

It is hoped that these stories will be picked up by teachers and used to teach children. They can serve as examples in guiding children to use the morals in their daily activities. By drawing their minds into thinking properly, their thinking power will be developed. This will prove invaluable in facing difficulties, unexpected circumstances and disasters, without being confused.

The stories teach valuable lessons to correct our current life style. For instance, the second story, "Finding a New Spring", teaches the value of perseverance. Today people who are enslaved to the modern development of science and technology, are lazy due to the easy availability of things they need (and things they don't need). They become used to giving up their efforts to achieve goals when there are even minor difficulties. They give up, change their minds, and try something else. Having become lazy, their thinking power declines, as does their effort to overcome difficulties. Consequently, they also do not understand how to solve the problems of living with others, and their human values decline as well.

Mankind has achieved the present level of civilization over a long period of time, by using vast human energy to control his weaknesses. Deep and immeasurable dedication and effort have been required to develop human physical and intellectual skills. We need to preserve these qualities for the future peace and happiness of the world.

Our highest efforts are needed to preserve declining human qualities and values. If not, the future will be a turmoil of quarrels and conflicts. Mature and compassionate people of diverse cultures are realizing this danger. The cause is the discouragement of the teaching of an internal moral code. Modern educators and psychologists have neglected the function of the moral development of children. This is the major cause of the worldwide increasing crime rate. Fifty years ago children were taught moral values, but there is no such subject in modern schools, while churches and temples are poorly attended. Without such teaching, where will a young child learn what is good and bad, from cartoons, commercials and movies? Why has this subject been neglected in the field of education and in the society at large?

In "Finding a New Spring", when the caravan lost its way, the leader did not blame others or grumble, he was determined to overcome the unexpected circumstances. In the midst of the weakened thinking of the others, he was the only one who could be depended on to lead the search for water. Even after tiring digging led to the great rock obstacle, he was not one to give up. His perseverance broke through the slab and reached the goal. How joyful they all were! Why do we not teach our children to follow such examples in their unexpected encounters? The adults who read these stories to children must point out morals like these and help them to develop their tender minds.

My deep gratitude and appreciation go to The Corporate Body of the Buddha Educational Foundation for funding the printing and distribution of this volume. And I thank all the others who have assisted in this work. That there are such people willing to contribute so unselfishly gives reason for optimism and hope in this world. May the merit they have earned cause their ultimate happiness.

May all beings be well and happy!

Kurunegoda Piyatissa
November 30, 1994

Buddhist Literature Society Inc.
New York Buddhist Vihara
84-32 124th Street
Kew Gardens
New York, N.Y. 11415, U.S.A.

Whatever in these retellings
has the ring of Truth
is given by
Todd S. Anderson
in memory of
an embodiment of compassion
Franklin F. Campbell MD
teacher and loving friend

From the Storyteller to the Listeners

When you read or listen to these very old stories, if you wonder how much is really true, the Buddha gave some advice that might help. He said that when you listen to what a monk says you should test the meaning, weigh or consider it, and depend on your own insides to know the truth of it. Then follow and practice what you know to be true.

Let us praise the Exalted, Worthy,
Fully Self-Enlightened One
and follow the Truth

1

Demons in the Desert
[The Correct Way of Thinking]
(Apaṇṇaka-Jātaka)[1]

At one time, when the Buddha was living in Jetavana monastery in Sāvatthi, his millionaire devotee Anāthapiṇḍika came with 500 friends who were followers of schools of thought other than the Buddha's. They listened to the Buddha's preaching, and became converted to his teachings. But when the Buddha left Sāvatthi for Rājagaha, they returned to their old practices. When the Buddha returned to Sāvatthi, they came in the company of Anāthapiṇḍika to visit the Buddha again. Anāthapiṇḍika at this time told the Buddha that in his absence, his friends had abandoned the Buddha's teachings. The Buddha then emphasized the value of the three gems [ratana-ttaya],[2] explaining their value and the value of the practice of the five precepts [pañca-sīla-s, the first five

---

1   Tradition says that this Jātaka story will be among the last to be forgotten when the Buddha's teachings disappear from the world at the end of our present aeon.

2   The three gems are the Buddha, the truth preached by the Buddha [Dhamma], and the Brotherhood founded by the Buddha [Saṅgha].

*sikkhā-pada-*s].[3] Further, he said that by believing bad advice instead of remaining steadfast with good advice such as his, people in the past fell prey to demons in a wilderness; whereas those who remained steadfast to such advice as his prospered in that same wilderness. And he became silent. Anāthapiṇḍika then requested the Buddha to disclose the past story. And the Buddha disclosed the story hidden by re-becoming in this way:

Once upon a time there were two merchants, who were friends. Both of them were getting ready for business trips to sell their merchandise, so they had to decide whether to travel together. They agreed that, since each had about 500 carts, and they were going to the same place along the same road, it would be too crowded to go at the same time.

One decided that it would be much better to go first. He thought, "The road will not be rutted by the carts, the bullocks will be able to choose the best of all the grass, we will find the best fruits and vegetables to eat, my people will appreciate my leadership and, in the end, I will be able to bargain for the best prices."

The other merchant considered carefully and realized there were advantages to going second. He thought, "My friend's carts will level the ground so we won't have to do any road work, his bullocks will eat the old rough grass and new tender shoots will spring up for mine to eat. In the same way, they will pick the old fruits and vegetables and fresh ones will grow for us to enjoy. I won't have to waste my time bargaining when I can take the price already set and make my profit." So he agreed to let his friend go first. This friend was sure he'd fooled him and gotten the best of him – so he set out first on the journey.

The merchant who went first had a troublesome time of it. They came to a wilderness called the 'Waterless Desert' [Nirudaka Kantāra], which the local people said was haunted by demons. When the caravan reached the middle of it, they met a large group coming from the opposite

---

3   The five precepts are not killing, not stealing, not committing adultery, not
     lying, and not intoxicating the mind.

direction. They had carts that were mud smeared and dripping with water. They had lotuses and water lilies in their hands and in the carts. The headman, who had a know-it-all attitude, said to the merchant, "Why are you carrying these heavy loads of water? In a short time you will reach that oasis on the horizon with plenty of water to drink and dates to eat. Your bullocks are tired from pulling those heavy carts filled with extra water – so throw away the water and be kind to your overworked animals!"

Even though the local people had warned them, the merchant did not realize that these were not real people, but demons in disguise. They were even in danger of being eaten by them. Being confident that they were helpful people, he followed their advice and had all his water emptied onto the ground.

As they continued on their way they found no oasis or any water at all. Some realized they'd been fooled by beings that might have been demons, and started to grumble and accuse the merchant. At the end of the day all the people were tired out. The bullocks were too weak from lack of water to pull their heavy carts. All the people and animals lay down in a haphazard manner and fell into a deep sleep. Lo and behold, during the night the demons came in their true frightening forms and gobbled up all the weak defenseless beings. When they were done there were only bones lying scattered around – not one human or animal was left alive.

After several months, the second merchant began his journey along the same way. When he arrived at the wilderness, he assembled all his people and advised them – "This is called the 'Waterless Desert' and I have heard that it is haunted by demons and ghosts. Therefore we should be careful. Since there may be poison plants and foul water, don't drink any local water without asking me." In this way they started into the desert.

After getting about halfway through, in the same way as with the first caravan, they were met by the water-soaked demons in disguise. They told them the oasis was near and they should throw away their water. But the wise merchant saw through them right away. He knew it didn't make sense to have an oasis in a place called 'Waterless Desert'. And besides, these people had bulging red eyes and an aggressive and pushy attitude, so he suspected they might be demons. He told them to leave them alone saying, "We are businessmen who don't throw away good water before we know where the next is coming from."

Then, seeing that his own people had doubts, the merchant said to them, "Don't believe these people, who may be demons, until we actually find water. The oasis they point to may be just an illusion or a mirage. Have you ever heard of water in this 'Waterless Desert'? Do you feel any rain-wind or see any storm clouds?" They all said, "No", and he continued, "If we believe these strangers and throw away our water, then later we may not have any to drink or cook with – then we will be weak and thirsty – it would be easy for demons to come and rob us, or even eat us up! Therefore, until we really find water, do not waste even a drop!"

The caravan continued on its way and, that evening, reached the place where the first caravan's people and bullocks had been killed and eaten by the demons. They found the carts and human and animal bones lying all around. They recognized that the fully loaded carts and the scattered bones belonged to the former caravan. The wise merchant told certain people to stand watch around the camp during the night.

The next morning the people ate breakfast, and fed their bullocks well. They added to their goods the most valuable things left from the first caravan. So they finished their journey very successfully, and returned home safely so that they and their families could enjoy their profits.

The Buddha then said further:

"The wise merchant and his followers were I who am today the Buddha and my present disciples. The foolish merchant and his followers were Devadatta and his disciples."

The moral: "One must always be wise enough not to be fooled by tricky talk and false appearances."

Finding a New Spring
[Perseverance]
(Vaṇṇupatha-Jātaka)

This story was delivered by the Buddha while he was living in Jetavana monastery in Sāvatthi with regard to a disheartened monk who became negligent when it came to meditation.

After meditating for five years in the forest and still not achieving any spiritual results, this monk decided to give up meditation, and he returned to Jetavana monastery to see the Buddha. On seeing him, the Buddha asked the reason for his coming to Jetavanārāma and questioned him as to why he gave up meditation in the forest. Further, he said, "In a previous life, by working hard you not only saved your life, but also the lives of your fellows in a caravan of 500 carts when in a sandy desert. So why now have you given up your efforts?"

The monk then asked the Buddha to disclose the ancient story. And the Buddha disclosed it in this way:

Once upon a time a certain tradesman was leading a caravan to another country to sell his goods. Along the way they came to the edge of a severe hot-sand desert. They asked about, and found that during the daytime the sun heats up the fine sand until it's as hot as charcoal, so no one can walk on it – not even bullocks or camels! So the caravan leader hired a desert guide, one who could follow the stars, so they could travel only at night when the sand cools down. They began the dangerous nighttime journey across the desert.

A couple nights later, after eating their evening meal, and waiting for the sand to cool, they started out again. Later that night the desert guide, who was driving the first cart, saw from the stars that they were getting close to the other side of the desert. He had also overeaten, so that when he relaxed, he dozed off to sleep. Then the bullocks who, of course, couldn't tell directions by reading the stars, gradually turned to the side and went in a big wide circle until they ended up at the same place they had started from!

By then it was morning, and the people realized they were back at the same spot they'd camped at the day before. They lost heart and began to cry about their condition. Since the desert crossing was supposed to be over by now, they had no more water and were afraid they would die of thirst. They even began to blame the caravan leader and the desert guide – "We can do nothing without water!", they complained.

Then the tradesman thought to himself, "If I lose courage now, in the middle of this disastrous situation, my leadership has no meaning. If I fall to weeping and regretting this misfortune, and do nothing, all these goods and bullocks and even the lives of the people, including myself, may be lost. I must be energetic and face the situation!" So he began walking back and forth, trying to think out a plan to save them all.

Remaining alert, out of the corner of his eye, he noticed a small clump of grass. He thought, "Without water, no plant could live in this desert." So he called over the most energetic of his fellow travelers and asked them to dig up the ground on that very spot. They dug and dug, and after a while they got down to a large stone. Seeing it they stopped, and began to blame the leader again, saying, "This effort is useless. We're just wasting our time!" But the tradesman replied, "No, no, my friends, if we give up the effort we will all be ruined and our poor animals will die – let us be encouraged!"

As he said this, he got down into the hole, put his ear to the stone, and heard the sound of flowing water. Immediately, he called over a boy who had been digging and said, "If you give up, we will all perish – so take this heavy hammer and strike the rock."

The boy lifted the hammer over his head and hit the rock as hard as he could – and he himself was the most surprised when the rock spilt in two and a mighty flow of water gushed out from under it! Suddenly, all the people were overjoyed. They drank and bathed and washed the animals and cooked their food and ate.

Before they left, they raised a high banner so that other travelers could see it from afar and come to the new spring in the middle of the hot-sand desert. Then they continued on safely to the end of their journey.

"At that time, the persevering boy who obtained water by splitting the rock was this monk. The people of the caravan were the Buddha's followers today. And the tradesman was I, myself, who have today become the Buddha."

The moral: "Don't give up too easily. Keep on trying until you reach the goal."

The Golden Plate
[Greed and Honesty]
(*Serivāṇija-Jātaka*)

A certain other monk also became very discouraged in his practice of meditation. The news of this was spread among the monks at the Jetavana monastery in Sāvatthi, and they discussed it one evening in the preaching hall. When the Buddha entered, he asked, "Oh monks, what were you talking about before I came?" The monks then told the Buddha about this monk. The Buddha said, "Oh monks, not only today, but even in the past, by not persevering with proper behavior such a monk became bound with anger from birth to birth." The monks then asked the Buddha to disclose the past story. And the Buddha then disclosed it in this way:

Once upon a time in a place called Seri, there were two salesmen of pots and pans and hand-made trinkets. They agreed to divide the town between them. They also said that after one had gone through his area, it was all right for the other to try and sell where the first had already been.

One day, while one of them was coming down a street, a poor little girl saw him and asked her grandmother to buy her a bracelet. The old grandmother replied, "How can we poor people buy bracelets?" The little girl said, "Since we don't have any money, we can give our black sooty old plate." The old woman agreed to give it a try, so she invited the dealer inside.

The salesman saw that these people were very poor and innocent, so he didn't want to waste his time with them. Even though the old woman pleaded with him, he said he had no bracelet that she could afford to buy. Then she asked, "We have an old plate that is useless to us. Can we trade it for a bracelet?" The man took it and, while examining it, happened to scratch the bottom of it. To his surprise, he saw that underneath the black soot, it was a golden plate! But he didn't let on that he had noticed it. Instead he decided to deceive these poor people so he could get the plate for next to nothing. He said, "This is not worth even one bracelet. There's no value in this. I don't want it!" He left, thinking he would return later when they would accept even less for the plate.

Meanwhile the other salesman, after finishing in his part of town, followed after the first as they had agreed. He ended up at the same house. Again the poor little girl begged her grandmother to trade the old plate for a bracelet. The woman saw that this was a nice tender looking merchant and thought, "He's a good man, not like the rough-talking first salesman." So she invited him in and offered to trade the same black sooty old plate for one bracelet. When he examined it, he too saw that it was pure gold under the grime. He said to the old woman, "All my goods and all my money together are not worth as much as this rich golden plate!"

Of course the woman was shocked at this discovery, but now she knew that he was indeed a good and honest fellow. So she said she would be glad to accept whatever he could trade for it. The salesman said, "I'll give you all my pots and pans and trinkets, plus all my money, if you will let me keep just eight coins and my balancing scale, with its cover to put the golden plate in." They made the trade. He went down to the river, where he paid the eight coins to the ferryman to take him across.

By then the greedy salesman had returned, already adding up huge imaginary profits in his head. When he met the little girl and her grandmother again, he said he had changed his mind and was willing to offer a few cents, but not one of his bracelets, for the useless black sooty old plate. The old woman then calmly told him of the trade she had just made with the honest salesman, and said, "Sir, you lied to us."

The greedy salesman was not ashamed of his lies, but he was saddened as he thought, "I've lost the golden plate that must be worth a hundred thousand." So he asked the woman, "Which way did he go?" She told him the direction. He left all his things right there at her door and ran down to the river, thinking, "He robbed me! He robbed me! He won't make a fool out of me!"

From the riverside he saw the honest salesman still crossing over on the ferryboat. He shouted to the ferryman, "Come back!" But the good merchant told him to keep on going to the other side, and that's what he did.

Seeing that he could do nothing, the greedy salesman exploded with rage. He jumped up and down, beating his chest. He became so filled with hatred towards the honest man, who had won the golden plate, that he made himself cough up blood. He had a heart attack and died on the spot!

The Buddha then concluded this Jātaka story by identifying the births.

"The foolish greedy salesman was Devadatta. The wise and good salesman was I who have today become the Buddha."[4]

The moral: "'Honesty is the best policy.'"

---

4   This is said to be the first time that Devadatta conceived a grudge against the Enlightenment Being.

The Mouse Merchant
[Diligence and Gratitude]
(Cullakaseṭṭhi-Jātaka, Cullaseṭṭhi-Jātaka)

When the Buddha was dwelling in the city of Rājagaha in the lay physician Jīvaka's mango grove, this Jātaka story was delivered by the Buddha on account of the elder Cullapanthaka.

In the city of Rājagaha, the chief millionaire's daughter had an affair with one of her young slaves. Later, she became pregnant. At that time, she said to the slave, "I have become pregnant. It is not good for us to stay here. Should my father and mother come to know of what we have done, they will kill us both. Let us run away from here." The young slave boy, though, postponing and postponing their departure, kept delaying it. In the meantime, one day the young girl went home when her lover was not there, gathered her things, and left. When the young boy came home, not seeing her, he chased after her. When it became dark, he met up with her at an inn, where she had just given birth to their child. The young boy said, "Now, we can no longer return home." Both agreed not to return to Rājagaha and to settle down away from her family, unbeknown to anyone. As the boy was born on the road, he was named Panthaka [Journeyman, One Born on the Road].

She then gave birth again, in the same way, while traveling on the road, but this time while going to see her parents. As this son, too, was born on the road, they called the elder son Mahāpanthaka [Big Panthaka] and this younger son Cullapanthaka [Little Panthaka]. When the two children had grown up, the millionaire's daughter sent them to her father asking him to give them a good education.

At their grandfather's home, they grew up to become young men, and they went with their grandfather to listen to the Buddha's sermons. As they used to go to listen to the Buddha often, the elder son, Mahāpanthaka, decided to become a monk. And obtaining permission from his grandparents, he became a monk. After a few years, when he reached the age of twenty, he received higher ordination. And after meditating for a few months, he attained Arahant-ship [sainthood through the eradication of one's cravings], and lived blissfully. Once that he had experienced the rapturous ecstasy of Arahant-ship, he thought, "Why should I not also share such an experience with my younger brother?" Thinking this, he got permission from his millionaire grandfather to give ordination to his younger brother as a novice. But because of a previous unwholesome deed that the younger brother had done in a past life, he could not learn by heart even a four-line stanza of the Law [Dhamma] over a period of four months. His elder brother then expelled him from the temple, saying, "As you have not been able to learn even a four-line stanza of the Law in four months, you cannot fulfill the discipline of a monk."

Cullapanthaka became very sad and thought, "Let me disrobe and return home, where I can practice charity and perform other good works as a lay householder." Thinking this, he left the temple early in the morning of the next day.

On that day, early in the morning, the omnipresent one was viewing the world with his divine eye, and he saw Cullapanthaka leaving the temple for home. He therefore alighted on the road, walking toward Cullapanthaka. When Cullapanthaka saw the Buddha, he went up to the Buddha and prostrating himself before the Buddha, to the Buddha's side, he told the Buddha what had happened to him. Hearing him the Buddha, knowing the whole story, told him not to worry and gave him a piece of clean white cloth. He asked him to repeat again and again these words while facing toward the rising sun: "Removal of impurity; removal of impurity." Advising him in this way, the Buddha left at the appointed time with 550 monks from the temple for lunch at the physician Jīvaka's house.

While the Venerable Cullapanthaka was repeating again and again the words the Buddha had told him to repeat, he was stroking over and over again the piece of clean white cloth that the Buddha had given him. While doing this, he realized the impermanence of all things in the world, he realized that everything in the world comes into being and then ceases existence, and he gained Arahant-ship.

At the same time as he had been stroking the cloth, the Buddha saw that Cullapanthaka was developing his mind with regard to impermanence. Seeing this, the Buddha uttered three stanzas regarding the changing nature of the world to be heard by Cullapanthaka only. Hearing these three stanzas, the Venerable Cullapanthaka attained Arahant-ship with the five higher knowledges [pañcābhiññā-s].

When Jīvaka offered the Buddha water before lunch as an invitation to eat, the Buddha put his hand over his bowl and asked a servant to go back to the temple to see whether or not there were still any monks there. Knowing this, the Venerable Cullapanthaka thought, "My elder brother, Mahāpanthaka, thought that there were no monks in the temple. Therefore, I will have to inform him that there are indeed monks here." Thinking this, he filled up the whole mango grove with monks through his miraculous powers [iddhi-vidhā-s]. Among them, some monks were stitching robes, some were dyeing robes, and some were repeating sacred texts by heart. The servant who went there to see whether or not there were still any monks in the temple saw a thousand monks in all sorts of activities. He returned and said that there were many monks in the mango grove. Then the Buddha asked that man to go back and say to those monks that the Buddha wants to summon the Venerable Cullapanthaka. The man returned to the temple and said this, and a thousand monks said, "I am Cullapanthaka. I am Cullapanthaka." The man then returned to the Buddha and told him of this. The Buddha then said, "Now go again, and take the hand of the first monk to say, 'I am Cullapanthaka.' All the others will then disappear." When the man did so, it happened in just this way. And the Venerable Cullapanthaka came with the man.

At the end of lunch, the Venerable Cullapanthaka delivered a sermon covering all Buddhist teachings [the entire *Tipiṭaka*, or Theravāda Buddhist canon].

This was discussed in the evening by the monks assembled in the preaching hall. At that time, the Buddha said, "Oh monks, just as Cullapanthaka has today thrived through religious teaching, just so in a previous birth Cullapanthaka prospered with wealth." Then the monks invited the Buddha to disclose the story of Cullapanthaka's past birth. The Buddha disclosed it in this way:

Once upon a time, an important adviser to a certain king [Cullakaseṭṭhi (Cullaseṭṭhi), 'The Younger Millionaire'] was on his way to a meeting with the king and other advisers. Out of the corner of his eye, he saw a dead mouse by the roadside. He said to those who were with him, "Even from such small beginnings as this dead mouse, an energetic young fellow could build a fortune. If he worked hard and used his intelligence, he could start a business and support a wife and family."

A passer-by [Cullantevāsika, 'The Junior Student'] heard the remark. He knew this was a famous adviser to the king, so he decided to follow his words. He picked up the dead mouse by the tail and went off with it. As luck would have it, before he had gone even a block, a shopkeeper stopped him. He said, "My cat has been pestering me all morning. I'll give you two copper coins for that mouse." So it was done.

With the two copper coins, he bought sweet cakes, and waited by the side of the road with them and some water. As he expected, some people who picked flowers for making garlands were returning from work. Since they were all hungry and thirsty, they agreed to buy sweet cakes and water for the price of a bunch of flowers from each of them. In the evening, the man sold the flowers in the city. With some of the money he bought more sweet cakes and returned the next day to sell to the flower pickers.

This went on for a while, until one day there was a terrible storm, with heavy rains and high winds. While walking by the king's pleasure garden, he saw that many branches had been blown off the trees and were lying all around. So he offered to the king's gardener that he would clear it all away for him, if he could keep the branches. The lazy gardener quickly agreed.

The man found some children playing in a park across the street. They were glad to collect all the branches and brush at the entrance to the pleasure garden, for the price of just one sweet cake for each child.

Along came the king's potter, who was always on the lookout for firewood for his glazing oven. When he saw the piles of wood the children had just collected, he paid the man a handsome price for it. He even threw into the bargain some of his pots.

With his profits from selling the flowers and the firewood, the man opened up a refreshment shop. One day all the local grass mowers, who were on their way into town, stopped in his shop. He gave them free sweet cakes and drinks. They were surprised at his generosity and asked, "What can we do for you?" He said there was nothing for them to do now, but he would let them know in the future.

A week later, he heard that a horse dealer was coming to the city with 500 horses to sell. So he got in touch with the grass mowers and told each of them to give him a bundle of grass. He told them not to sell any grass to the horse dealer until he had sold his. In this way he got a very good price.

Time passed until one day, in his refreshment shop, some customers told him that a new ship from a foreign country had just anchored in the port. He saw this to be the opportunity he had been waiting for. He thought and thought until he came up with a good business plan.

First, he went to a jeweler friend of his and paid a low price for a very valuable gold ring, with a beautiful red ruby in it. He knew that the foreign ship was from a country that had no rubies of its own, where gold too was expensive. So he gave the wonderful ring to the captain of the ship as an advance on his commission. To earn this commission, the captain agreed to send all his passengers to him as a broker. He would then lead them to the best shops in the city. In turn, the man got the merchants to pay him a commission for sending customers to them.

Acting as a middleman in this way, after several ships came into port, the man became very rich. Being pleased with his success, he also remembered that it had all started with the words of the king's wise adviser. So he decided to give him a gift of 100,000 gold coins. This was half his entire wealth. After making the proper arrangements, he met with the king's adviser and gave him the gift, along with his humble thanks.

The adviser was amazed, and he asked, "How did you earn so much wealth to afford such a generous gift?" The man told him it had all started with the adviser's own words not so long ago. They had led him to a dead mouse, a hungry cat, sweet cakes, bunches of flowers, storm damaged tree branches, children in the park, the king's potter, a refreshment shop, grass for 500 horses, a golden ruby ring, good business contacts, and finally a large fortune.

Hearing all this, the royal adviser thought to himself, "It would not be good to lose the talents of such an energetic man. I too have much wealth, as well as my beloved only daughter. As this man is single, he deserves to marry her. Then he can inherit my wealth in addition to his own, and my daughter will be well cared for."

This all came to pass, and after the wise adviser died, the one who had followed his advice became the richest man in the city. The king appointed him to the adviser's position. Throughout his remaining life, he generously gave his money for the happiness and well-being of many people.

The Buddha then said:

"This man [Cullantevāsika] became the Venerable Cullapanthaka. And the king's adviser who had seen the dead mouse [Cullakaseṭṭhi (Cullaseṭṭhi) was I who have become the Buddha."

The moral: "With energy and ability, great rewards come even from small beginnings."

5

The Price Maker
[Foolishness]
(Taṇḍulanāḷi-Jātaka)

When the Buddha was living in Jetavana monastery, the Venerable Lāludāyi got into a quarrel with the Venerable Dabba Mallaputta, and on this account the Buddha disclosed this Jātaka story.

When the Venerable Dabba Mallaputta was distributing tickets for households at which the different monks could get lunch, on some days Venerable Dabba Mallaputta would give some monks tickets for choice alms and some monks tickets for inferior alms. On other days, he would give other monks the tickets for choice alms and other monks the tickets for the inferior alms. When a ticket for the inferior alms would come to Lāludāyi, he would start an uproar. One day, the Venerable Dabba Mallaputta just gave the box of tickets to the Venerable Lāludāyi and said, "From now on, you distribute the tickets." From that time on, the Venerable Lāludāyi distributed the tickets for lunch. But, he did not know which tickets were for the choice lunch and which tickets were for the inferior lunch. Since he did not know what to do, he distributed the different tickets at random to the various monks, regardless of their status in the Order [Saṅgha]. Because of this, many young monks who in ordinary circumstances would be given tickets for choice lunches, complained, and arguments followed. Because elderly monks who could not digest rich foods were being given tickets for choice lunches, and young monks were being given tickets for lunches at the homes of the infirm who were preparing simpler fare, the monks were becoming discouraged and complained about going for alms to their allotted locations. So, one day the younger monks took the ticket box from Lāludāyi, saying, "You can no longer do this!" And there was an uproar.

The Buddha heard the noise and asked Ānanda about it. On being told what it was about, the Buddha said, "Not only today, but even in the past, Lāludāyi has robbed people of their gainfulness through his ignorance." The Venerable Ānanda then asked the Buddha how it was in the past. And the Buddha disclosed the Jātaka story of *Taṇḍulanāḷi*, this story about a measure of dry rice.

Long ago and far away, there was a king who ruled in Benares, in northern India. One of his ministers was called the Royal Price Maker, and he was a very honest man. His job was to set a fair price for anything the king wanted to buy or sell.

On some occasions, the king did not like his price making. He did not get as big a profit as he wanted. He did not want to pay so much when he bought, or sell for what he thought was not enough. So he decided to change the price maker.

One day he saw a nice-looking young man and he thought, "This fellow will be good for my price making position." So he dismissed his former honest price maker, and appointed this man to be the new one. The man thought, "I must make the king happy by buying at very low prices and selling at very high prices." So he made the prices ridiculous, without caring at all what anything was worth. This gained the greedy king a lot of money, and made him very happy. Meanwhile, all the others who dealt with the new price maker, including the king's other ministers and ordinary people, became very unhappy.

Then one day a horse merchant arrived in Benares with 500 horses to sell. There were stallions, mares and colts. The king invited the merchant to the palace, and called upon his Royal Price Maker to set a price for all 500 horses. Thinking only of pleasing the king, he said, "The entire herd of horses is worth one cup of rice." So the king ordered that one cup of rice be paid to the horse dealer, and all the horses were taken to the royal stables.

Of course the merchant was very upset, but he could do nothing at the moment. Later he heard about the former price maker, who had a reputation for being very fair and honest. So he approached him and told him what had happened. He wanted to hear his opinion, in order to get a proper price from the king. The former price maker said, "If you do as I say, the king will be convinced of the true value of the horses. Go back to the price maker and satisfy him with a valuable gift. Ask him to tell the value of one cup of rice, in the presence of the king. If he agrees, come and tell me. I will go with you to the king."

Following this advice, the merchant went to the price maker and gave him a valuable gift. The gift made him very happy, so that he saw the value of pleasing the horse dealer. Then the merchant said to him, "I was very happy with your previous evaluation. Can you please convince the king of the value of one cup of rice?" The foolish price maker said, "Why not? I will explain the worth of one cup of rice, even in the presence of the king."

So the price maker thought the horse dealer was satisfied with his cup of rice. He arranged for another meeting with the king, as the merchant was departing for his own country. The merchant reported back to the old price maker, and they went together to see the king.

All the king's ministers and his full court were in the royal meeting hall. The horse merchant said to the king, "My lord, I understand that in this your country, my whole herd of 500 horses is worth one cup of rice. Before I leave for home, I want to know the value of one cup of rice in your country." The king turned to his loyal price maker and said, "What is the value of one cup of rice?"

The foolish price maker, in order to please the king, had previously priced the herd of horses at one cup of rice. Now, after receiving a bribe from the horse dealer, he wanted to please him too. So he replied to the king, in his most dignified manner, "Your worship, one cup of rice is worth the city of Benares, including even your own harem, as well as all the suburbs of the city. In other words, it is worth the whole kingdom of Benares!"

On hearing this, the royal ministers and wise men in the assembly hall started to roar with laughter, slapping their sides with their hands. When they calmed down a little, they said, "Earlier we heard that the kingdom was priceless. Now we hear that all Benares, with its palaces and mansions, is worth only a cup of rice! The decision of the Royal Price Maker is so strange! Where did your highness find such a man? He is good only for pleasing a king such as you, not for making fair prices for a merchant who sells his horses from country to country."

Hearing the laughter of his whole court, and the words of his ministers and advisers, the king was ashamed. So he brought back his former price maker to his official position. He agreed to a new fair price for the herd of horses, as set by the honest price maker. Having learned a lesson, the king and his kingdom lived justly and prospered.

The Buddha, having ended this story, said:

"Lāludāyi was the foolish price maker. And the honest price maker was I who have become the fully enlightened one."

The moral: "A fool in high office can bring shame even to a king."

6

Prince Goodspeaker and the Water Demon
(Devadhamma-Jātaka)

When the Buddha was living in Jetavana monastery, he told this story about a monk who still possessed a great deal of wealth.

A wealthy man of Sāvatthi, after his wife had died, wanted to join the Buddha's order and build a temple while keeping all his possessions. In his temple, he set up a pantry and a kitchen, and he stocked his pantry with ghee, rice and other foodstuffs. He then would have his servants cook for him whatever food he desired.

As he was well provided with the various requisites for life, for his enjoyment he would from time to time have the things in his room rearranged so that he could see them all in a different light. One day, he took out all his robes and other cloth items such as bedspreads, towels and curtains, and spread them outside in the sunshine so as to dry them from the humidity. While these were drying outside, some wandering monks on pilgrimage passed by. Seeing these things, they asked to whom they belonged. The wealthy monk said that they belonged to him. The passing by monks said, "Oh friend, it is not good to have more than three robes. That is how the Buddha advised us. It is not good for one's monkhood to have all these possessions."[5] Saying this, they took him with them and went to see the Buddha, telling the Buddha about this. The Buddha said, "Oh monk, why did you retain all your worldly goods?" And he told him of the disadvantages of retaining such lay wealth.

The wealthy monk then got angry and, taking off his upper robe, he threw it on the ground. Without any shame or fear, standing only wearing

---

5   The three allowed robes for a monk are a two plied outer robe, a two-part dress robe, and a bottom skirt robe worn underneath the two part dress robe.

his skirt robe, he said, "Then I will go about like this all the time."

Then the Buddha said, "Was it not you who in the past spent twelve years searching for shame and fear of sin? Then how it that now, after vowing to follow the teachings of the Buddha, you have flung off your robes and stand here devoid of shame?"

Hearing this, the wealthy monk put on his upper robe again.

The other monks who were there, then asked the Buddha to relate the old story. And the Buddha related it.

Chapter 1. Rebirth of the Bodhisatta

Once upon a time, there was a very righteous king. He had a lovely queen who gave birth to a beautiful baby. This made the king very happy. He decided to give his son a name that might help him in later life. So he called him Prince Goodspeaker [Mahiṁsāsa].

It just so happened that the prince was no ordinary baby. This was not his first life or his first birth. Millions of years before, he had been a follower of a long-forgotten teaching 'Buddha' – a fully 'Enlightened One'. He had wished with all his heart to become a Buddha just like his beloved master.

He was reborn in many lives – sometimes as poor animals, sometimes as long-living gods and sometimes as human beings. He always tried to learn from his mistakes and develop the 'Ten Perfections' [*dasa-pāramitā-s*].[6] This was so he could purify his mind and remove the three root causes of unwholesomeness [*akusala-mūla*-s] – the poisons of craving, anger and the delusion of a separate self. By using the Perfections, he would someday be able to replace the poisons with the three purities [*ti-pārisuddhi*-s] – nonattachment [*alobha*], loving-kindness [*adosa*] and wisdom [*amoha*].

This 'Great Being' had been a humble follower of the forgotten Buddha. His goal was to gain the same enlightenment of a Buddha – the experience of complete Truth. So people call him 'Bodhisatta', which

6   The Ten Perfections are giving (or liberality), morality, renunciation, wisdom, energy, patience, truthfulness, resolution, loving-kindness, and equanimity.

means 'Enlightenment Being'. No one really knows about the millions of lives lived by this great hero. But many stories have been told – including this one about a prince called Goodspeaker. After many more rebirths, he became the Buddha who is remembered and loved in all the world today.

Chapter 2. The Teaching of the Gods

In time, the queen gave birth to another son, who was named Prince Moon [Canda]. Shortly after both children began walking about, their mother suddenly became very sick, and died.

To help him look after his playful children, the king found a princess to become his new queen. In a few years, this queen gave birth to a beautiful bright little boy. He was named Prince Sun [Suriya]. Since the king was so happy, he wanted to please his queen, and reward her for bringing up all three children. So he promised to grant her one wish. The queen considered, and said, "Thank you my lord. I will make my wish at some time in the future."

As time went on, the three princes grew into wonderful playful youngsters. The queen saw that Prince Goodspeaker was intelligent and understanding. She thought, "If these two older princes remain in the palace, my son, Prince Sun, will never get a chance to be king. Therefore, I must do something to make him the next king."

One day, when the king was in a good mood, the queen respectfully approached him and reminded him of the promised wish. He was very happy and said, "Ask whatever you want!" The queen said, "Oh my husband and king, grant that after the course of your life is over, my son, Prince Sun, will be the next king."

The king was shocked by this request. He became angry and said, "My first two children are like bright stars! How can I give the kingdom to my third son? All the people will blame me. That cannot be done!" The queen kept silent.

As happy as the king had been, he now became just as unhappy. He was afraid and filled with doubt. He suspected that the queen might destroy his first-born children by some wicked means. He decided that he must make sure his children were safe.

Secretly, the king called Prince Goodspeaker and Prince Moon to him. He told them of the queen's dangerous desire. He sadly said that the only safe thing for them to do was to leave the kingdom. They should return only after their father's death, and take their rightful places ruling the kingdom. The two obedient princes accepted their father's order and prepared to leave.

In a few days they were ready. They said their sad good-byes to their father and friends, and left the palace. On their way through the royal gardens, they came upon Prince Sun. He had always been very affectionate and friendly towards his two older half-brothers. He was upset to hear that they were leaving for a very long time. So he decided that he too would leave the kingdom. The three friendly princes departed together.

For several months they traveled, until they reached the forest country of the mighty Himalayas. They were very tired and sat down under a tree. The oldest brother, Prince Goodspeaker, said to the youngest, Prince Sun, "Please go down to the nearby lake and fill some lotus leaves with water. Bring them back here so we all can drink."

They did not know that the beautiful dark blue lake was possessed by a water demon! He was permitted by his demon ruler [Vessavaṇa] to eat any beings that he could convince to go into the water. There was also one condition. He could not eat anyone who knew the answer to the question, "What is the teaching of the gods?"

When Prince Sun arrived at the shore of the lake, being dry and dirty and tired, he went directly into the water without any investigation. Suddenly the water demon rose up from under the water and captured him. He asked him, "What is the teaching of the gods?" Prince Sun said, "I know the answer to that! The sun and the moon are the teachings of the gods." "*You* don't know the teaching of the gods, so you belong to *me*!", said the water demon. Then he pulled Prince Sun under the water and locked him up in a deep cave.

Since Prince Sun was delayed, Prince Goodspeaker asked the second brother, Prince Moon, to go down to the lake and bring back water in lotus leaves. When he got there, he too went directly into the water without examining. Again the water demon appeared, grabbed him, and asked, "What is the teaching of the gods?" Prince Moon said, "I know the answer to that! The four directions – North, East, South and West – these are the teachings of the gods." "*You* don't know the teaching of the gods, so you belong to *me*!", replied the water demon. Then he locked up Prince Moon in the same underwater cave with Prince Sun.

When both his brothers did not return, Prince Goodspeaker began to worry that they might be in some danger. So he himself went down to the beautiful dark blue lake. As he was a wise and careful person, he did not go directly into the water. Instead, he investigated and saw that there were two sets of footprints leading into the lake – but not coming out again! To protect himself, he got his sword and bow and arrows ready. He began to walk around the lake.

Seeing that this prince did not go straight into the lake, the water demon appeared to him disguised as a humble villager. He said to him, "My dear friend, you look tired and dirty from much walking. Why don't you get into the water and bathe, drink, and eat some lotus roots?"

Remembering the one-way footprints, Prince Goodspeaker said, "You must be some kind of demon disguised as a human! What have you done with my brothers?" Surprised at being recognized so quickly, the water demon returned to his true ferocious appearance. He replied to the wise prince, "By my rights, I have captured your brothers!"

The prince asked, "For what reason?" "So that soon I can gobble them up!", the demon answered. "I have permission from my demon ruler to eat all those who go into this lake who do not know the teaching of the gods. If anyone does know the teaching of the gods, I am not allowed to eat him."

The Prince asked, "Why do you need to know this? What is the advantage to a demon like you, to know the teaching of the gods?" The water demon replied, "I know there must be some advantage to me." "Then I will tell you what the gods teach," said Prince Goodspeaker. "But I have a problem. Look at me. I am covered with dust and dirt from traveling. I cannot speak about wise teachings in this condition."

By now, the water demon realized that this prince was especially wise. So he washed and refreshed him. He gave him water to drink from lotus leaves, and tender lotus roots to eat. He prepared a comfortable seat for him, decorated with pretty wildflowers. After laying aside his sword and bow and arrows, the Enlightenment Being sat on the adorned seat. The ferocious demon sat by his feet, just like a student listening to a respected teacher.

Prince Goodspeaker said, "This is the teaching of the gods:
You should be ashamed to do unwholesome deeds.
You should be afraid to do unwholesome deeds.
You should always do wholesome deeds – that bring happiness to others, and help mankind.
Then you will shine with the inner light of calm and peacefulness."

The water demon was pleased with this answer, and said, "Worthy prince, you have completely satisfied my question. You have made me so happy that I will give you back one of your brothers. Which one do you choose?"

Prince Goodspeaker said, "Release my younger brother, Prince Sun." To this the demon replied, "My lord prince, wise one, you know the teaching of the gods but you do not practice it!" The prince asked, "Why do you say that?" The demon said, "Because you leave the older one to die, and save the younger. You do not respect elders!"

The prince then said, "Oh demon, I know the teaching of the gods, and I do practice it. We three princes came to this forest because of the youngest brother. His mother requested our father's kingdom for him. So it was for our protection that our father sent us here. The young Prince Sun joined us out of friendship. But if we return to the court without him, and say he was eaten by a water demon who wanted to know the teaching of the gods, who would believe us? They would think we killed him because he was the cause of our danger. This would bring shame to us and unhappiness to the kingdom. Fearing such unwholesome results, I tell you again to release the young Prince Sun."

The water demon was so pleased with this answer that he said, "Well done, well done, my lord. You know the true teaching of the gods, and you do practice that true teaching. I will gladly give back both your brothers!" So saying, he went down into the lake and brought both princes back to shore. They were wet, but unharmed.

Later on, the Bodhisatta gave further helpful advice to the demon. He said, "Oh water demon, my new friend, you must have done many unwholesome deeds [*akusala-kamma*-s] in your previous lives, so that you were born as a flesh-eating demon. And if you continue in this way, you will be trapped in a terrible state even in later lives. For unwholesome deeds lead to shame, fear and unpleasant rebirth. But wholesome deeds [*kusala-kamma*-s] lead to self-respect, peace and pleasant rebirth. Therefore, it would be much better for you to do pure deeds, rather than impure deeds, from now on." This turned the demon from his past ways, and the princes lived together happily under his protection.

One day, word came that the king had died. So the three princes, as well as their friend the water demon, returned to the capital city. Prince Goodspeaker was crowned as king. Prince Moon became the chief minister, and Prince Sun became commander of the army. The water demon was awarded a safe place to live, where he was well fed, cared for and entertained for the rest of his life. In this way they all acquired wholesome meritorious thoughts, leading to rebirth in a heaven world.

* * *

"The well-to-do monk who abandoned shame in the presence of the Buddha was the water demon. Prince Sun was the Venerable Ānanda. Prince Moon was the Venerable Sāriputta. And Prince Goodspeaker was I who have become the Buddha."

In this way, the Buddha connected this Jātaka story with the events of his day.

The moral: "Unwholesome actions bring shame and fear. Wholesome actions bring self-respect and peace."

Little Prince No-father
[The Power of Truth]
(Kaṭṭhahāri-Jātaka)[7]

When the Buddha was living in the Jetavana monastery he disclosed this story on Vāsabhakkhattiyā's account. The full story will be found in the twelfth book in the *Bhaddasāla-Jātaka* [No. 465].

Vāsabhakkhattiyā was the daughter of the Sakyā king Mahānāma by a slave girl named Nāgamuṇḍā. However, she later became the chief queen of the king of Kosala, King Pasenadi. After their marriage, she gave birth to a lovely son by him, whom they named Viḍūḍabha. Only later did King Pasenadi find out that Vāsabhakkhattiyā was the daughter of a slave girl. Once he knew this, he deprived Vāsabhakkhattiyā and Viḍūḍabha of their royalty. They continued to live in the palace, though, but without the help of any servants and without any respect.

The Buddha, on hearing this news, came to visit King Kosala with a retinue of 500 followers. After sitting down in the seat that was prepared for him, he asked the king of Kosala why Vāsabhakkhattiyā had been deprived of her royal status. After hearing what the king had to say with regard to this, the Buddha said, "Your lordship, she is the daughter of King Mahānāma. She is wed to you, a king. She has bore you, a king, a son. Therefore, why does he not deserve to inherit your realm? In ancient times, a king gave sovereignty over his kingdom to a son who was the issue of a casual relationship with a young maiden who just collected firewood."

---

7   This story would seem to be related to that of Śakuntalā and King Duṣyanta in the great Indian *Mahābhārata* epic, which story is the basis for Kālidāsa's famous play about "Śakuntalā and the Token of Recognition" (more properly, "The Story of Śakuntalā by means of a Token of Recognition").

The king then asked the Buddha to disclose the story. And the Buddha disclosed it in this way:

Once upon a time, the King of Benares went on a picnic in the forest. The beautiful flowers and trees and fruits made him very happy. As he was enjoying their beauty, he slowly went deeper and deeper into the forest. Before long, he became separated from his companions and realized that he was all alone.

Then he heard the sweet voice of a young woman. She was singing as she collected firewood. To keep from being afraid of being alone in the forest, the king followed the sound of the lovely voice. When he finally came upon the singer of the songs, he saw that she was a beautiful fair young woman, and immediately fell in love with her. They became very friendly, and the king became the father of the firewood woman's child.

Later, he explained how he had gotten lost in the forest, and convinced her that he was indeed the King of Benares. She gave him directions for getting back to his palace. The king gave her his valuable signet ring, and said, "If you give birth to a baby girl, sell this ring and use the money to bring her up well. If our child turns out to be a baby boy, bring him to me along with this ring for recognition." So saying, he departed for Benares.

In the fullness of time, the firewood woman gave birth to a cute little baby boy. Being a simple shy woman, she was afraid to take him to the fancy court in Benares, but she saved the king's signet ring.

In a few years, the baby grew into a little boy. When he played with the other children in the village, they teased him and mistreated him, and even started fights with him. It was because his mother was not married that the other children picked on him. They yelled at him, "No-father! No-father! Your name should be No-father [Apitika]!"

Of course this made the little boy feel ashamed and hurt and sad. He often ran home crying to his mother. One day, he told her how the other children called him, "No-father! No-father! Your name should be No-father!" Then his mother said "Don't be ashamed, my son. You are not just an ordinary little boy. Your father is the King of Benares!"

The little boy was very surprised. He asked his mother, "Do you have any proof of this?" So she told him about his father giving her the signet ring, and that if the baby was a boy she should bring him to Benares, along with the ring as proof. The little boy said, "Let's go, then!" Because of what happened, she agreed, and the next day they set out for Benares.

When they arrived at the king's palace, the gatekeeper told the king the firewood woman and her little son wanted to see him. They went into the royal assembly hall, which was filled with the king's ministers and advisers. The woman reminded the king of their time together in the forest. Finally she said, "Your majesty, here is your son."

The king was ashamed in front of all the ladies and gentlemen of his court. So, even though he knew the woman spoke the truth, he said, "He is not my son!" Then the lovely young mother showed the signet ring as proof. Again the king was ashamed and denied the truth, saying, "It is not my ring!"

Then the poor woman thought to herself, "I have no witness and no evidence to prove what I say. I have only my faith in the power of truth." So she said to the king, "If I throw this little boy up into the air, if he truly is your son, may he remain in the air without falling. If he is not your son, may he fall to the floor and die!"

Suddenly, she grabbed the boy by his foot and threw him up into the air. Lo and behold, the boy sat in the cross-legged position, suspended in mid-air, without falling. Everyone was astonished, to say the least! Remaining in the air, the little boy spoke to the mighty king. "My lord, I am indeed a son born to you. You take care of many people who are not related to you. You even maintain countless elephants, horses and other animals. And yet, you do not think of looking after and raising me, your own son. Please do take care of me and my mother."

Hearing this, the king's pride was overcome. He was humbled by the truth of the little boy's powerful words. He held out his arms and said, "Come to me my son, and I will take good care of you."

Amazed by such a wonder, all the others in the court put out their arms. They too asked the floating little boy to come to them. But he went directly from mid-air into his father's arms. With his son seated on his lap, the king announced that he would be the crown prince, and his mother would be the number one queen.

In this way, the king and all his court learned the power of truth. Benares became known as a place of honest justice. In time the king died. The grown up crown prince wanted to show the people that all deserve respect, regardless of birth. So he had himself crowned under the official name, "King No-father [King Apitika; or King Kaṭṭhavāhana, 'One Who Carries Firewood']!" He went on to rule the kingdom in a generous and righteous way.

The Buddha then identified the births in this way:

"The mother in those days was Queen Mahāmāyā. The father was King Suddhodana. And 'King No-Father' [*i.e.*, King Kaṭṭhavāhana] was I who am today the Buddha."

The moral: "The truth is always stronger than a lie."

The One-Hundredth Prince
[Obedience to a Wise Teacher]
(Gāmaṇī-Jātaka)

No. 8. When the Buddha was living in Jetavana monastery, he disclosed this story on account of a monk who had given up his attempt to attain final emancipation from the cycle of re-becoming [saṁsāra]. Both the background to this story, and the story itself, are told in the eleventh book in connection with the Saṁvara-Jātaka [No. 462].

[No. 462. There was once a person who lived in Sāvatthi who heard the Buddha and, his mind being pleased, he became a monk. After this, he fulfilled his duties to his master[8] for five years. He learned what he needed to know for successful meditation, and then he left to live alone and meditate. He went to the countryside of Kosala. There he came to a remote village. The villagers, seeing the monk's calm demeanor, were greatly pleased. They asked him to stay in their village, and they made a shelter for him. They invited him to spend the rainy season retreat there

Observing the rainy season retreat there for the whole three months, he strove to meditate, but he could not gain any results. He thought, "The Buddha taught us that there are four different types of people who are smart in different ways. I am one who can teach the Pāli language. Therefore, what is the use of staying in this remote village."

Giving up his efforts to meditate, he went back to Sāvatthi to stay there, to look upon the Buddha's beauty and to listen to the Buddha's sweet words. He went to Jetavana monastery and he saw his teacher, his master and others whom he knew before. When they asked why he had

---

8   A master is an elderly teacher of one's teacher.

returned, he said that he had given up his effort to obtain Nibbāna (final release from all existence). They all reproached him, and he was taken to see the Buddha.

The Buddha asked him, "Oh monk, why did you give up your efforts? In my teaching, it is not possible for a lazy person to attain the goal of Arahant-ship (sainthood through the eradication of one's cravings). But in one of your previous lives, you exerted great effort." And at the request of the monks, the Buddha told the past story.]

This is how it was:

Once upon a time, there was a king who had one hundred sons. The youngest, the one-hundredth, was Prince Gāmaṇi ['Village Headman'].[9] He was very energetic, patient and kind.

All the princes were sent to be taught by teachers. Prince Gāmaṇi, even though he was the one-hundredth in line to the throne, was lucky enough to have the best teacher. He had the most learning and was the wisest of them of all. He was like a father to Prince Gāmaṇi, who liked, respected and obeyed him.

In those days, it was the custom to send each educated prince to a different province. There he was to develop the country and help the people. When Prince Gāmaṇi was old enough for this assignment, he went to his teacher and asked which province he should request. He said, "Do not select any province. Instead, tell your father the king that if he sends you, his one-hundredth son, out to a province, there will be no son remaining to serve him in his home city." Prince Gāmaṇi obeyed his teacher, and pleased his father with his kindness and loyalty.

Then the prince went again to his teacher and asked, "How best can I serve my father and the people, here in the capital city?" The wise teacher replied, "Ask the king to let you be the one to collect fees and taxes, and distribute benefits to the people. If he agrees, then carry out your duties honestly and fairly, with energy and kindness."

9　In Jātaka No. 462, this young prince's name is Saṁvara.

Again the prince followed his teacher's advice. Trusting his one-hundredth son, the king was glad to assign these functions to him. When he went out to perform the difficult task of collecting fees and taxes, the young prince was always gentle, fair and lawful. When he distributed food to the hungry, and other necessary things to the needy, he was always generous, kind and sympathetic. Before long, the one-hundredth prince gained the respect and affection of all.

Eventually, the king came to be on his deathbed. His ministers asked him who should be the next king. He said that all his one hundred sons had a right to succeed him. It should be left up to the citizens.

After he died, all the citizens agreed to make the one-hundredth prince their next ruler. Because of his goodness, they crowned him King Gāmaṇī the Righteous.

When the ninety-nine older brothers heard what had happened, they thought they had been insulted. Filled with envy and rage, they prepared for war. They sent a message to King Gāmaṇī, which said, "We are all your elders. Neighbor countries will laugh at us if we are ruled by the one-hundredth prince. Either you give up the kingdom or we will take it by war!"

After he received this message, King Gāmaṇī took it with him to his wise old teacher, and asked his advice.

It just so happened that this honorable gentle teacher was the re-born Enlightenment Being. He said, "Tell them you refuse to wage war against your brothers. Tell them you will not help them kill innocent people you have come to know and love. Tell them that, instead, you are dividing the king's wealth among all one hundred princes. Then send each one his portion." Again the king obeyed his teacher.

Meanwhile, the ninety-nine older princes had brought their ninety-nine small armies to surround the royal capital. When they received the king's message and their small portions of the royal treasure, they held a meeting. They decided that each portion was so small it was almost meaningless. Therefore, they would not accept them.

But then they realized that, in the same way, if they fought with King Gāmaṇī and then with each other, the kingdom itself would be divided into small worthless portions. Each small piece of the once great kingdom would be weak in the face of any unfriendly country. So, led by Uposatha, the eldest brother, they sent back their portions of the royal treasure as offerings of peace, and accepted the rule of King Gāmaṇī.

The king was pleased, and invited his brothers to the palace to celebrate the peace and unity of the kingdom. He entertained them in the most perfect ways – with generosity, pleasant conversation, providing instruction for their benefit, and treating all with even-handed courtesy.

In this way the king and the ninety-nine princes became closer as friends than they had been as brothers. They were strong in their support of each other. This was known in all the surrounding countries, so no one threatened the kingdom or its people. After a few months, the ninety-nine brothers returned to their provinces.

King Gāmaṇi the Righteous invited his wise old teacher to live in the palace. He honored him with great wealth and many gifts. He held a celebration for his respected teacher, saying to the full court, "I, who was the one-hundredth prince, among one hundred worthy princes, owe all my success to the wise advice of my generous and understanding teacher. Likewise, all who follow their wise teachers' advice will earn prosperity and happiness. Even the unity and strength of the kingdom, we owe to my beloved teacher."

The kingdom prospered under the remainder of the generous and just rule of King Gāmaṇi the Righteous.

At the end of the Buddha's disclosing this story, the monk who had been discouraged gained emancipation [Arahant-ship].

The Buddha identified the births in this way:

"At that time, this monk was the great King Gāmaṇi. Sāriputta was Prince Uposatha. The elders and secondary elders were the other brothers. The Buddha's followers were the country's citizens. And I myself was the wise teacher who advised the king."

The moral: "One is rewarded a hundred-fold for following the advice of a wise teacher."

9

The King With One Gray Hair
[Ordination]
(Makhādeva-Jātaka)

One evening when the Buddha was living in Jetavana monastery, the monks assembled in the preaching hall were talking about the Buddha's renunciation. When the Buddha came there, he asked, "Oh monks, what were you talking about before I came?" The monks mentioned the splendidness of the Buddha's renunciation. The Buddha then said, "Oh monks, not only today, but even in the past I have renounced my royal life. The monks then invited the Buddha to disclose the old story of his past renunciation.

The Buddha said:

A very, very long time ago, there were people who lived much longer than they do today. They lived many thousand years. At that time, the Enlightenment Being was born as a baby named Makhādeva. He lived 84,000 years as a child and crown prince. At the time of our story, he had been a young king for 80,000 years.

One day, Makhādeva told the royal barber, "If you see any gray hair on my head, you must tell me immediately!" Of course, the barber promised to do so.

Another 4,000 years passed, until Makhādeva had been a young king for 84,000 years. Then one day, while he was cutting the king's hair, the royal barber saw just one little gray hair on all the king's head. So he said, "Oh my lord, I see one gray hair on your head." The king said, "If this be so, pull it out and put it in my hand." The barber got his golden tweezers, plucked out the single little gray hair, and put it in the king's hand.

At that time, the king still had at least another 84,000 years left to live as an old king! Looking at the one gray hair in his hand, he became very afraid of dying. He felt like death was closing in on him, as if he were

trapped in a burning house. He was so afraid, that the sweat rolled down his back, and he shuddered.

King Makhādeva thought, "Oh foolish king, you have wasted all this long life and now you are near death. You have made no attempt to destroy your greed and envy, to live without hating, and to get rid of your ignorance by learning the truth and becoming wise."

As he thought this, his body burned and the sweat kept rolling down. Then he decided once and for all, "It is time to give up the kingship, be ordained as a monk, and practice meditation!" Thinking so, he granted the income of a whole town to the barber. It amounted to one hundred thousand per year.

Then the king called his oldest son to him and said, "My son, I have seen a gray hair. I have become old. I have enjoyed the worldly pleasures of great wealth and power. When I die, I want to be reborn in a heaven world, to enjoy the pleasures of the gods. So I will be ordained as a monk. You must now take the responsibility of ruling the country. I will live the life of a monk in the forest."

Hearing of this, the royal ministers and the rest of the court rushed to the king and said, "Our lord, why do you suddenly want to be ordained?"

The king held up the gray hair in his hand and said, "My ministers and subjects, I have realized that this gray hair shows that the three stages of life – youth, middle age and old age – are coming to an end. This first gray hair was the messenger of death sitting on my head. Gray hairs are like angels sent by the god of death. Therefore, this very day is the time for me to be ordained."

The people wept at the news of his departure. King Makhādeva gave up his royal life, went into the forest, and was ordained as a monk. There he practiced what holy men call the 'Four Heavenly States of Mind' [*cattāri-brahma-vihāra*-s]. First is loving-kindness, tender affection for all [*mettā*]. Second is feeling sympathy and pity for all those who suffer [*karuṇā*]. Third is feeling happiness for all those who are joyful [*muditā*]. And the fourth state is balance and calm, even in the face of difficulties or troubles [*upekkhā*].

After 84,000 years of great effort meditating and practicing these states as a humble forest monk, the Bodhisatta died. He was reborn in a high heaven world, to live a life a million years long!

The Buddha said:

"In those days, the Venerable Ānanda was the barber. The king's son was Rāhula. And I myself was King Makhādeva."

The moral: "Even a long life is too short to waste."

10

The Happy Monk
[Joys of the Spiritual Life]
(Sukhavihāri-Jātaka)

When the Buddha was dwelling in the Anūpiya mango grove, he told this story about the elder Bhaddiya.

In the days of the elder Bhaddiya's royalty, he lived in constant fear in the palace. Now, after his gaining Arahant-ship [emancipation], he was living without fear. Because of this, he would go about saying, "What happiness! Oh, what happiness! This is happiness, indeed!" The monks mentioned this to the Buddha. And the Buddha said, "Oh monks, not only today, but even in the past Bhaddiya spoke like this as well." And the monks requested the Buddha to tell the story of the bygone days. The Buddha related it in this way:

Once upon a time, there was a high-class rich man. As he became older, he realized that the suffering of old age was about the same for rich and poor alike. So he gave up his wealth and class position, and went into the forest to live as a poor monk. He practiced meditation and developed his mind. He freed himself from unwholesome thoughts, and became contented and happy. His peacefulness and friendliness gradually drew 500 followers to his side.

At that time, long ago, most monks usually looked pretty serious. But there was one monk who, even though he was quite dignified, always wore at least a little smile. No matter what happened, he never lost this glimmer of inner happiness. And on happy occasions, he had the broadest smile and the warmest laughter of all.

Sometimes monks, as well as others, would ask him why he was so happy that he always wore a smile. He chuckled and said, "If I told you,

you wouldn't believe me! And if you thought I spoke a lie, it would be a dishonor to my master." The wise old master knew the source of the happiness that could not be wiped from his face. He made this happiest monk his number one assistant.

One year, after the rainy season, the old monk and his 500 followers went to the city. The king permitted them to live in his pleasure garden for the springtime.

This king was a good man, who took his responsibilities as ruler seriously. He tried to protect the people from danger, and increase their prosperity and welfare. He always had to worry about neighboring kings, some of whom were unfriendly and threatening. He often had to make peace between his own rival ministers of state.

Sometimes his wives fought for his attention, and for the advancement of their sons. Occasionally, a dissatisfied subject even threatened the life of the king himself! And of course, he had to worry constantly about the finances of the kingdom. In fact, he had so much to worry about, that he never had time to be happy!

As summer approached, he learned that the monks were preparing to return to the forest. Considering the health and welfare of the old leader, the king went to him and said, "Your reverence, you are now very old and weak. What good does it do to go back to the forest? You can send your followers back, while you remain here."

The chief monk then called his number one assistant to him and said, "You are now to be the leader of the other monks, while you all live in the forest. As I am too old and weak, I will remain here as offered by the king." So the 500 returned to the forest and the old one remained.

The number one assistant continued practicing meditation in the forest. He gained so much wisdom and peace that he became even happier than before. He missed the master, and wanted to share his happiness with him. So he returned to the city for a visit.

When he arrived, he sat on a rug at the feet of the old monk. They didn't speak very much, but every so often the number one assistant would say, "What happiness! Oh, what happiness!"

Then the king came to visit. He paid his respects to the chief monk. However, the one from the forest just kept saying, "What happiness! Oh, what happiness!" He did not even stop to greet the king and show proper respect. This disturbed him, and he thought, "With all my worries, as busy as I am looking after the kingdom, I take time out for a visit and this monk does not respect me enough to even recognize me. How insulting!" He said to the senior of the two monks, "Venerable sir, this monk must be stupid from overeating. That must be why he is so full of happiness. Does he lie around here so lazy all the time?"

The head monk replied, "Oh king, have patience and I will tell you the source of his happiness. Not many know it. He was once a king, just as rich and mighty as you! Then he was ordained a monk and gave up his kingly life. Now he thinks his old happiness was nothing compared to his present joy!

"He used to be surrounded by armed men, who guarded and protected him. Now, sitting alone in the forest with nothing to fear, he has no need for armed guards. He has given up the burden of worrying about wealth that has to be protected. Instead, free of the worry of wealth and the fear of power, his wisdom protects himself and others. He advances in meditation to such inner peace, that he cannot keep from saying, 'What happiness! Oh, what happiness!'"

The king understood at once. Hearing the story of the happy monk made him feel at peace. He stayed for a while and received advice from both of them. Then he honored them, and returned to the palace.

Later the happy monk, who once had been a king, paid his respects to his master and returned to the lovely forest. The old chief monk lived out the remainder of his life, died, and was reborn in a high heaven world.

"Bhaddiya was the number one assistant in those days. And the wise old master was I who have today become the fully enlightened one."

The moral: "Unattached to wealth and power, happiness increases."

11

Beauty and Gray
[A Wise Leader]
(Lakkhaṇa-Jātaka, Lakkhaṇamiga-Jātaka)

When the Buddha was living in the Bamboo Grove monastery near Rājagaha, he related this story with regard to Devadatta.

Devadatta had created a schism among the monks by taking away 500 monks from the Buddha to dwell at Gayāsīsa. When the Buddha, through his divine eye, saw that these monks were ready to attain emancipation [Arahant-ship], he asked the Venerable Moggallāna and Sāriputta to go to preach to them and, satisfying them by their preaching, to bring them back. Going to Gayāsīsa, they brought all 500 monks back to the Bamboo Grove monastery.

One evening, the other monks were talking about this incident in the preaching hall. When the Buddha came, they told him about what they had been talking. The Buddha said, "Not only today, but even in the past Sāriputta has gained glory by bringing back his kinsfolk, while Devadatta has lost his following." The assembled monks then invited the Buddha to tell the old story. And the Buddha related it in this way:

Once upon a time, there was a deer who was the leader of a herd of a thousand. He had two sons. One was very slim and tall, with bright alert eyes, and smooth reddish fur. He was called Beauty [Lakkhaṇa]. The other was gray in color, also slim and tall, and was called Gray [Kāḷa].

One day, after they were fully grown, their father called Beauty and Gray to him. He said, "I am now very old, so I cannot do all that is necessary to look after this big herd of deer. I want you, my two grown up children, to be the leaders, while I retire from looking after them all the time. We will divide the herd, and each of you will lead 500 deer." So it was done.

In India, when the harvest time comes, the deer are always in danger. The rice is at its tallest, and the deer cannot help but go into the paddies and eat it. To avoid the destruction of their crops, the human beings dig pits, set sharp stakes in the ground, and build stone traps – all to capture and kill the deer.

Knowing this was the season, the wise old deer called the two new leaders to him. He advised them to take the herds up into the mountain forest, far from the dangerous farmlands. This was how he had always saved the deer from being wounded or killed. Then he would bring them back to the low lands after the harvest was over.

Since he was too old and weak for the trip, he would remain behind in hiding. He warned them to be careful and have a safe journey. Beauty set out with his herd for the mountain forest, and so did Gray with his.

The villagers all along the way knew that this was the time the deer moved from the low-lying farmlands to the high countryside. So they hid along the way and killed the deer as they passed by.

Gray did not pay attention to his father's wise advice. Instead of being careful and traveling safely, he was in a hurry to get to the lush mountain forest. So he moved his herd constantly, during the night, at dawn and dusk, and even in broad daylight. This made it easy for the people to shoot the deer in Gray's herd with bows and arrows. Many were killed, and many were wounded, only to die in pain later on. Gray reached the forest with only a few deer remaining alive.

The tall, sleek, red-furred Beauty, was wise enough to understand the danger to his moving herd. So he was very careful. He knew it was safer to stay away from the villages, and from all humans. He knew it was not safe in the daytime, or even at dawn or dusk. So he led his herd wide around the villages, and moved only in the middle of the night. Beauty's herd arrived in the mountain forest safe and sound, with no one killed or injured.

The two herds found each other, and remained in the mountains until well after the harvest season was over. Then they began the return to the farmland country.

Gray had learned nothing from the first trip. As it was getting cold in the mountains, he was in a hurry to get to the warmer low lands. So he was just as careless as before. Again the people hid along the way and attacked and killed the deer. All Gray's herd were killed, later to be eaten or sold by the villagers. Gray himself was the only one who survived the journey.

Beauty led his herd in the same careful way as before. He brought back all 500 deer, completely safe. While the deer were still in the distance, the old chief said to his doe, "Look at the deer coming back to us. Beauty has all his followers with him. Gray comes limping back alone, without his whole herd of 500. Those who follow a wise leader, with good qualities, will always be safe. Those who follow a foolish leader, who is careless and thinks only of himself, will fall into troubles and be destroyed."

After some time, the old deer died and was reborn as he deserved. Beauty became chief of the herd and lived a long life, loved and admired by all.

The Buddha then related the births in this way:

"In the past, when they were born as deer, Gray was Devadatta and Beauty was the elder Sāriputta. Beauty's followers are today the Buddha's followers. The mother doe was the mother of Rāhula. The father deer was I who am today the Buddha."

The moral: "A wise leader puts the safety of his followers first."

12

King Banyan Deer
(*Nigrodhamiga-Jātaka, Nigrodha-Jātaka*)[10]

This story was delivered by the Buddha while he was living in Jetavana monastery on account of the Venerable Kumāra Kassapa's mother.

In the city of Rājagaha there was a very wealthy millionaire who possessed a great deal of all sorts of the possessions and provisions that laymen ordinarily might acquire.

He had a daughter who had the spiritual good fortune to be able to attain Arahant-ship [emancipation, sainthood] in her very same lifetime. When she came of age, and her understanding of life was that of a mature woman, she asked her father for permission to become a nun. Both her father and mother refused her the permission saying that the family had much wealth, and if she became a nun there would be no heirs to whom to leave it. She made this request over and over again, and each time she was given the same response. Her parents were unable to get her to stop such requests, and without her permission they arranged for her to be married to an eligible young man from a nearby village.

After her marriage the girl, whose only interest was in gaining merit, spent her time practicing generosity, virtuousness and meditation. She had little interest in her wifely duties. In due course, though, she became pregnant without being aware of it. But, as she constantly requested of her husband, as well, permission to become a nun, he eventually decided to let her do so. She went to the nearby temple, which happened to belong to Devadatta, and there she was ordained. She was very happy there.

---

10 This story is depicted in the sculpture at the famous 2nd c. B.C.E. *stūpa* at Bhārhut in northern India.

As time passed, the other nuns noticed that she seemed to be pregnant. They asked her, "Are you pregnant?" She said that she was not aware of that, and that she was virtuous. But a rumor that she was indeed pregnant was spread about, and eventually it reached Devadatta. Devadatta summoned her and saw for himself that she was pregnant. Without any mercy, Devadatta expelled her from the order, saying that she would bring disgrace to his following.

She became very upset, and she went to see the Buddha. The Buddha understood, with his divine knowledge, what had happened to her. But, for the sake of avoiding blame being placed on anyone, he appointed a committee composed of reliable lay people, including the virtuous lady Visākhā and the millionaire Anāthapiṇḍika, and the like. The Buddha requested that they examine her, and report back as to whether she was pregnant before her ordination, or became pregnant after it.

They examined her, screening her from being seen by all the people in the hall, and declared that she was blameless. Later, when the child was born the king of Kosala, Pasenadi, brought him up. The child's name was Kumāra Kassapa. Eventually he, too, became ordained and attained Arahant-ship.

The Buddha said, "Not only in this life, even in a previous life as well, I have come to this woman's rescue in a similar situation." And everyone present asked the Buddha to disclose the past story.

The Buddha disclosed the story in this way:

Chapter 1. Compassion

Once upon a time, an unusual and beautiful deer was born in the forests near Benares, in northern India. Although he was as big as a young colt, it was easy for his mother to give birth to him. When he opened his eyes, they were as bright as sparkling jewels. His mouth was as red as the reddest forest berries. His hoofs were as black as polished coal. His little horns glistened like silver. And his color was golden, like a perfect summer's dawn. As he grew up, a herd of 500 deer gathered around him, and he became known as King Banyan Deer [Nigrodha].

Meanwhile, not far away, another beautiful buck deer was born, just as splendidly golden in color. In time, a separate herd of 500 deer came to follow him, and he was known as Branch Deer [Sākha].

The King of Benares at that time was very fond of eating venison. So he regularly hunted and killed deer. Each time he hunted, he went to a different village and ordered the people to serve him. They had to stop what they were doing, whether plowing or harvesting or whatever, and work in the king's hunting party.

The people's lives were upset by these interruptions. They grew fewer crops, and other businesses also had less income. So they came together and decided to build a large deer park for the king, at Benares. There he could hunt by himself, with no need to command the services of the villagers.

So the people built a deer park. They made ponds where the deer could drink, and added trees and grasses for them to eat from. When it was ready, they opened the gate and went out into the nearby forests. They surrounded the entire herds of Banyan and Branch deer. Then, with sticks and weapons and noisemakers, they drove them all into the deer park trap, and locked the gate behind them.

After the deer had settled down, the people went to the king and said, "Our crops and income have suffered because of your hunting requirements. Now we have made you a pleasant safe deer park where you can hunt by yourself, as you like. With no need of our aid, you can enjoy both the hunting and the eating of deer."

The king went to the new deer park. There he was pleased to see the vast herds. While watching them, his eye was caught by the two magnificent golden deer, with large fully-grown antlers. Because he admired their unusual beauty, the king granted immunity to these two alone. He ordered that they should be completely safe. No one could harm or kill them.

Once a day the king would come and kill a deer for his dinner table. Sometimes, when he was too busy, the royal cook would do this. The body would then be brought to the chopping block to be butchered for the oven.

Whenever the deer saw the bow and arrows, they went into a panic, trembling for their lives. They ran around wildly, some being injured and some wounded, many suffering great pain.

One day, King Banyan Deer's herd gathered around him. He called Branch Deer, and the two herds joined for a meeting. King Banyan Deer addressed them. "Although in the end, there is no escape from death, this needless suffering due to injuries and wounds can be prevented. Since the king only wishes the meat of one deer per day, let one be chosen by us each day to submit himself to the chopping block. One day from my herd, and the next day from Branch Deer's herd, the victim's lot will fall to one deer at a time."

Branch Deer agreed. From then on, the one whose turn it was, meekly surrendered himself and laid his neck on the block. The cook came each day, simply killed the waiting victim, and prepared the king's venison.

One day, the turn fell by chance to a pregnant doe in Branch Deer's herd. Caring for the others as well as herself and the unborn one, she went to Branch Deer and said, "My lord, I am pregnant. Grant that I may live until I have delivered my fawn. Then we will fill two turns rather than just one. This will save a turn, and thereby a single life for one long day."

Branch Deer replied, "No, no, I cannot change the rules in midstream and put your turn upon another. The pregnancy is yours; the babe is your responsibility. Now leave me."

Having failed with Branch Deer, the poor mother doe went to King Banyan Deer and explained her plight. He replied gently, "Go in peace. I *will* change the rules in midstream and put your turn upon another."

And the deer king went to the executioner's block, and laid down his own golden neck upon it.

A silence fell in the deer park. And some who tell this story even say that silence also fell in other worlds not seen from here.

Soon the royal cook came to kill the willing victim on the block. But when he saw it was one of the two golden deer the king had ordered spared, he was afraid to kill him. So he went and told the King of Benares.

The king was surprised, so he went to the park. He said to the golden deer, still lying on the block, "Oh king of deer, did I not promise to spare your life? What is the reason you come here like the others?"

King Banyan Deer replied, "Oh king of men, this time a pregnant doe was unlucky enough to be the one to die. She pleaded for me to spare her, for the sake of others as well as her unborn baby and herself. I could not help but feel myself in her place, and feel her suffering. I could not help but weep, to think the little one would never see the dawn, would never taste the dew. And yet, I could not force the pain of death on another, relieved to think it was not his turn today. So, mighty king, I offer my life for the sake of the doe and her unborn fawn. Be assured there is no other reason."

The King of Benares was overwhelmed. Powerful as he was, a tear rolled down his cheek. Then he said, "Oh great lord, the golden king of deer, even among human beings, I have not seen any such as you! Such great compassion, to share in the suffering of others! Such great generosity, to give your life for others! Such great kindness and tender love for all your fellow deer! Arise. I decree that you will never be killed by me or anyone else in my kingdom. And so too, the doe and her babe."

Without yet raising his head, the golden one said, "Are only we to be saved? What of the other deer in the park, our friends and kin?" The king said, "My lord, I cannot refuse you. I grant safety and freedom to all the deer in the park." "And what of the deer outside the park, will they be killed?" asked Banyan. "No my lord, I spare all the deer in my whole kingdom."

Still the golden deer did not raise up his head. He pleaded, "So the deer will be safe. But what will the other four-footed animals do?" "My lord, from now on they too are safe in my land." "And what of the birds? They too want to live." "Yes, my lord, the birds too will be safe from death at the hands of men." "And what of the fish, who live in the water?"

"Even the fish will be free to live, my lord." So saying, the King of Benares granted immunity from hunting and killing to all the animals in his land.

Having pleaded for the lives of all creatures, the Great Being arose.

Chapter 2. Teaching

Out of compassion and gratitude, King Banyan Deer – the Enlightenment Being, taught the King of Benares. He advised him to climb the five steps of training [*pañca-sīla*-s, the first five *sikkhā-pada*-s], in order to purify his mind.[11] He described them by saying, "It will benefit you, if you give up the five unwholesome actions [*akusala-kamma*-s]. These are:

– destroying life, for this is not compassion;

– taking what is not given, for this is not generosity;

– doing wrong in sexual ways, for this is not loving- kindness;

– speaking falsely, for this is not Truth;

---

11 The *pañca-sīla*-s, or 'five rules of morality,' are the first five of the ten (*dasa-*) *sikkhā-pada*-s, or 'steps of training.' The lay Buddhist community is supposed to observe these five at all times.

– losing your mind from alcohol, for this leads to falling down the first four steps."

He further advised him to do wholesome actions [*kusala-kamma-s*] that would bring happiness in this life and beyond.[12] Then King Banyan Deer, and both herds, returned to the forest.

In the fullness of time, the pregnant doe, who had stayed with Banyan's herd, gave birth to a fawn. He was as beautiful as a lotus blossom given as an offering to the gods.

When the fawn had grown into a young buck deer, he began playing with Branch Deer's herd. Seeing this, his mother said to him, "Better to die after a short life with the great compassionate one, than to live a long life with an ordinary one." Afterwards, her son lived happily in the herd of King Banyan Deer.

The only ones left unhappy, were the farmers and villagers of the kingdom. For, given total immunity by the king, the deer began to fearlessly eat the people's crops. They even grazed in the vegetable gardens inside the villages and the city of Benares itself!

So the people complained to the king, and asked permission to kill at least some of the deer as a warning. But the king said, "I myself promised complete immunity to King Banyan Deer. I would give up the kingship before I would break my word to him. No one may harm a deer!"

When King Banyan Deer heard of this, he said to all the deer, "You should not eat the crops that belong to others." And he sent a message to the people. Instead of making fences, he asked them to tie up bunches of leaves as boundaries around their fields. This began the Indian custom of marking fields with tied up leaves, which have protected them from deer to this very day.

Both King Banyan Deer and the King of Benares lived out their lives in peace, died, and were reborn as they deserved.

---

12 The *kusala-kamma-s* are the opposite of the *akusala-kamma-s*. These first five of the ten (*dasa-*) *kusala-kamma-s* are the same as the *pañca-sīla-s*, or 'five rules of morality,' which are also the first five of the ten *sikkhā-pada-s*, 'steps of training.'

* * *

When the Buddha finished relating this story, he preached the Four Noble Truths [*cattāri ariya-saccāni*], that life is by nature full of sorrow, the cause of sorrow is craving, it can only be stopped by stopping craving, this can only be done by practicing disciplined and moral conduct culminating in the life of concentration and meditation of a Buddhist monk.

The Buddha then connected the past story with the present:

"At that time in the past, Branch Deer was Devadatta, the pregnant doe was this nun, and the fawn was the young monk Kumāra Kassapa. King Banyan Deer was I who have in this life become the Buddha."

The moral: "Wherever it is found, compassion is a sign of greatness."

13

Mountain Buck and Village Doe
[Infatuation]
(Kaṇḍina-Jātaka)

When the Buddha was living in Jetavana monastery, he disclosed this story on account of a monk who wished to disrobe. The circumstances of its narration will be told in full in the *Indriya-Jātaka* [No. 423].

Before this monk was ordained, he had a wife. And after his ordination, he missed her and wasted his time constantly thinking about her instead of meditating. This was mentioned to the Buddha, and the Buddha summoned this monk and asked him, "Are you still infatuated with your former wife?" The monk said, "Yes." The Buddha said, "Even in one of your past lives, you came to ruin because of this woman. And now you are trying to do the same thing again." The monks present said, "Bhante, the past story is known to you, but we do not know it. Please disclose it to us." And the Buddha related the story:

Once upon a time, in northern India, there was a herd of village deer. They were used to being near villages; they were born there and grew up there. They knew they had to be very careful around people. This was especially true at harvest time, when the crops were tall, and the farmers trapped and killed any deer who came near.

At harvest time, the village deer stayed in the forest all day long. They only came near the village during the dark of the night. One of these was a beautiful young doe. She had soft reddish-brown fur, a fluffy white tail and big wide bright eyes.

During this particular season, there was a young mountain buck who had strayed into the same low forest. One day, he saw the beautiful young doe, and immediately became infatuated with her. He didn't know anything about her. But he imagined himself to be deeply in love with her, just because of her reddish-brown fur and her fluffy white tail and her big wide bright eyes. He even dreamed about her, although she did not know he existed!

After a few days, the young mountain buck decided to introduce himself. As he was walking out into the clearing where she was grazing, he was entranced by her appearance and could not take his eyes off her. He began speaking: "Oh my sweet beauty, as lovely as the stars and as bright as the moon, I confess to you that I am deeply –" Just then the young buck's hoof got caught in a root, he tripped and fell, and his face splashed in a mud puddle! The pretty village doe was flattered, so she smiled. But inside, she thought this mountain buck was really rather silly!

Meanwhile, unknown to the deer, there was a clan of tree fairies living in that part of the forest. They had been watching the mountain buck, while he secretly watched the village doe. When he walked out into the clearing, began his speech, and fell in the mud puddle – the fairies laughed and laughed. "What fools these dumb animals are!" they cried.

But one fairy did not laugh. He said, "I fear this is a warning of danger to this young fool!"

The young buck was a little embarrassed, but he did not see it as any kind of warning. From then on, he followed the doe wherever she went. He kept telling her how beautiful she was and how much he loved her. She didn't pay much attention.

Then night came, and it was time for the doe to go down to the village. The people who lived along the way knew the deer passed by at night. So they set traps to catch them. That night a hunter waited, hiding behind a bush.

Carefully, the village doe set out. The mountain buck, who was still singing her praises, went right along with her. She stopped and said to him, "My dear buck, you are not experienced with being around villages. You don't know how dangerous human beings are. The village, and the way to it, can bring death to a deer even at night. Since you are so young and inexperienced (and she thought to herself, 'and foolish'), you should not come down to the village with me. You should remain in the safety of the forest."

At this, the tree fairies applauded. But of course, the deer could not hear them.

The young buck paid no attention to the doe's warning. He just said, "Your eyes look so lovely in the moonlight!" and kept walking with her. She said, "If you won't listen to me, at least be quiet!" He was so infatuated with her, that he could not control his mind. But he did finally shut his mouth!

After a while, they approached the place where the hunter was hiding behind a bush. The fairies saw him, and became agitated and frightened for the deer's safety. They flew nervously around the tree branches, but they could only watch.

The doe could smell the hiding man. She was afraid of a trap. So, thinking to save her own life, she let the buck go first. She followed a little way behind.

When the hunter saw the unsuspecting mountain buck, he shot his arrow and killed him instantly. Seeing this, the terrified doe turned tail and ran back to the forest clearing as fast as she could.

The hunter claimed his kill. He started a fire, skinned the deer, cooked some of the venison and ate his fill. Then he threw the carcass over his shoulder and carried it back home to feed his family.

When the fairies saw what happened, some of them cried. As they watched the hunter cut up the once noble- looking buck, some of them felt sick. Others blamed the careful doe for leading him to the slaughter.

But the wise fairy, who had given the first warning, said, "It was the excitement of infatuation that killed this foolish deer. Such blind desire brings false happiness at first, but ends in pain and suffering."

The Buddha said:

"The young mountain buck who was killed was this monk. The doe at that time was the woman with whom this monk is infatuated. The wise fairy who witnessed this was I who am today the fully enlightened one."

The moral: "Infatuation leads to destruction."

14

The Wind-deer and the Honey-grass
[The Craving for Taste]
(*Vātamiga-Jātaka*)

At one time, when the Buddha was dwelling in the Bamboo Grove temple at Rājagaha, a very wealthy young man named Prince Tissa Kumāra went to hear the Buddha preach. Being pleased with the Buddha's teaching, he wanted to become a monk. The Buddha told him that he had to get the permission of his parents to be ordained. But his parents did not wish to give him the permission to become ordained as a monk since they had a lot of wealth with no one other than this son to leave it to. The young man then spent seven days without eating or drinking until he was at last given the permission to become a monk. After his ordination, he was known to everyone as Cullapiṇḍapātika Tissa (Cullapiṇḍapātiya Tissa), and he went with the Buddha to Jetavana temple in Sāvatthi when the Buddha returned there after a short while.

When the time of the New Year's festival arrived his parents, seeing the fine clothing that their son used to wear during this festival, began to weep. Their weeping was heard by a passing-by wandering slave girl who then asked the parents why they were crying. They explained to her what had happened, and she said that she would bring their son back to them.

Then the slave girl went to the city of Sāvatthi and rented an apartment in the area where the newly ordained monk would go for alms. She began to give him tasty and well-prepared alms on a regular basis, and in due course she persuaded the monk to disrobe. After a short time, the two of them went back to Rājagaha.

This became well-known among the community of monks, and even the Buddha learned of it. The Buddha said, "Oh monks, not only today, but even in the past this monk fell into the power of this woman through his attachment to taste." The monks said, "Oh Bhante, you know the old story, but we do not know it. Please tell it to us." And the Buddha disclosed the story in this way:

Once upon a time, the King of Benares, who was the Enlightenment Being, had a gardener [Sañjaya] who looked after his pleasure garden. Animals sometimes came into the garden from the nearby forest. The gardener complained about this to the king, who said, "If you see any strange animal, tell me at once."

One day, he saw a strange kind of deer at the far end of the garden. When he saw the man, he ran like the wind. That is why they are called 'wind-deer' [*vāta-miga*-s]. They are a rare breed, that are extremely timid. They are very easily frightened by human beings.

The gardener told the king about the wind-deer. He asked the gardener if he could catch the rare animal. He replied, "My lord, if you give me some bee's honey, I could even bring him into the palace!" So the king ordered that he be given as much bee's honey as he wanted.

This particular wind-deer loved to eat the flowers and fruits in the king's pleasure garden. The gardener let himself be seen by him little by little, so he would be less frightened. Then he began to smear honey on the grass where the wind-deer usually came to eat. Sure enough, the deer began eating the honey-smeared grass. Soon he developed a craving for the taste of this 'honey-grass'. The craving made him come to the garden every day. Before long, he would eat nothing else!

Little by little, the gardener came closer and closer to the wind-deer. At first, he would run away. But later, he lost his fear and came to think the man was harmless. As the gardener became more and more friendly, eventually he got the deer to eat the honey-grass right out of his hand. He continued doing this for some time, in order to build up his confidence and trust.

Meanwhile, the gardener had rows of curtains set up, making a wide pathway from the far end of the pleasure garden to the king's palace. From inside this pathway, the curtains would keep the wind-deer from seeing any people that might scare him.

When all was prepared, the gardener took a bag of grass and a container of honey with him. Again he began hand-feeding the wind-deer when he appeared. Gradually, he led the wind-deer into the curtained off pathway. Slowly, he continued to lead him with the honey-grass, until finally the deer followed him right into the palace. Once inside, the palace guards closed the doors, and the wind-deer was trapped. Seeing the people of the court, he suddenly became very frightened and began running around, madly trying to escape.

The king came down to the hall and saw the panic-stricken wind-deer. He said, "What a wind-deer! How could he have gotten into such a state? A wind-deer is an animal who will not return to a place where he has so much as seen a human, for seven full days. Ordinarily, if a wind-deer is at all frightened in a particular place, he will not return for the whole rest of his life! But look! Even such a shy wild creature can be enslaved by his craving for the taste of something sweet. Then he can be lured into the center of the city and even inside the palace itself.

"My friends, the teachers warn us not to be too attached to the place we live, for all things pass away. They say that being too attached to a small circle of friends is confining and restricts a broad outlook. But see how much more dangerous is the simple craving for a sweet flavor, or any other taste sensation. See how this beautiful shy animal was trapped by my gardener, by taking advantage of his craving for taste."

Not wishing to harm the gentle wind-deer, the king had him released into the forest. He never returned to the royal pleasure garden, and he never missed the taste of honey-grass.

When the Buddha had finished relating this story, he said:

"The gardener at that time is today the slave girl. The wind-deer was the monk named Cullapiṇḍapātika Tissa. And the king of Benares was I who have today become the fully enlightened one."

The moral: "'It is better to eat to live, than to live to eat.'"

15

The Fawn Who Played Hooky
[Truancy]
(Kharādiya-Jātaka)

The Buddha told this story when he was dwelling in Jetavana temple on account of a disobedient monk. These are the circumstances of its telling.

There was a certain monk who did not like to pay attention to anyone, and who was disobedient. Accordingly, when the Buddha saw him at one time, the Buddha asked him, "Oh monk, is it true what is being said about you, that you are disobedient and will not listen to anyone?" The monk said, "Yes, Bhante." The Buddha then said, "Oh monk, in the past you met your death because of your disobedience." The monks who were present then requested that the Buddha disclose the former story. And the Buddha did so. This is how it was:

Once upon a time, there was a herd of forest deer. In this herd was a wise and respected teacher, cunning in the ways of deer. He taught the tricks and strategies of survival to the young fawns.

One day, his younger sister [Kharādiyā] brought her son to him, to be taught what is so important for deer. She said, "Oh brother teacher, this is my son. Please teach him the tricks and strategies of deer." The teacher said to the fawn, "Very well, you can come at this time tomorrow for your first lesson."

At first, the young deer came to the lessons as he was supposed to. But soon, he became more interested in playing with the other young bucks and does. He didn't realize how dangerous it could be for a deer who learned nothing but deer games. So he started cutting classes. Soon he was playing hooky all the time.

Unfortunately, one day the fawn who played hooky stepped in a snare and was trapped. Since he was missing, his mother worried. She went to her brother the teacher, and asked him, "My dear brother, how is my son? Have you taught your nephew the tricks and strategies of deer?"

The teacher replied, "My dear sister, your son was disobedient and un-teachable. Out of respect for you, I tried my best to teach him. But he did not want to learn the tricks and strategies of deer. He played hooky! How could I possibly teach him? You are obedient and faithful, but he is not. It is useless to try to teach him."

Later they heard the sad news. The stubborn fawn who played hooky had been trapped and killed by a hunter. He skinned him and took the meat home to his family.

The Buddha said:

"The fawn was this disobedient monk. The wise deer's sister was the nun Uppalavaṇṇā. And I, myself, who have today become the Buddha, was the wise teacher deer."

The moral: "Nothing can be learned from a teacher by one who misses the class."

16

The Fawn Who Played Dead
[Attendance]
(*Tipallatthamiga-Jātaka, Sikkhākāma-Jātaka*)

This story was told by the Buddha when he was dwelling in Badārika temple in Kosambī. The circumstances of its narration are as follows:

Once, when the Buddha was dwelling in the Aggāḷava temple, after the Buddha would preach in the evening, the monks and people who came to hear the Buddha's sermon would fall asleep in the preaching hall. During the night, the snoring and grinding of teeth of some would disturb the others, and they complained about this to one another. On account of this, the Buddha forbade anyone to sleep in the preaching hall. He then returned to Kosambī.

The Venerable Rāhula, the Buddha's son, after listening to the Buddha's sermon, because of this, had no place to sleep, not wishing to violate the Buddha's precept. So Rāhula passed the night in the outhouse made available for the Buddha's use. In the morning, when the Buddha went to the outhouse, before entering, he coughed so as to make a sound, "*Ahaṁ* [I am (here)]". And Rāhula responded in like manner, "*Ahaṁ*." Then the Buddha asked, "Who is it who has just coughed, '*Ahaṁ*'?" And Rāhula told him who it was. The Buddha asked, "Why are you in the outhouse?" And Rāhula told him that he was there since the Buddha had forbade anyone from passing the night in the preaching hall. Then the Buddha summoned the monks and modified his precept. He said, "Should Rāhula who is my son be treated like this, how will other youths who wish to join the order be treated! Such treatment will not retain them."

That evening, the monks gathered in the preaching hall were discussing Rāhula's goodness and diligence in following the rules set down. As they were talking, the Buddha entered. On hearing what the monks were talking about, he said, "Rāhula has always been diligent in following rules. It was like this also in a former re-becoming as an animal." The monks then asked the Buddha to relate the past story. And the Buddha told the story of the past.

Once upon a time, there was a herd of forest deer. In this herd was a wise and respected teacher, cunning in the ways of deer. He taught the tricks and strategies of survival to the young fawns.

One day, his younger sister brought her son [Rāhula] to him, to be taught what is so important for deer. She said, "Oh brother teacher, this is my son. Please teach him the tricks and strategies of deer." The teacher said to the fawn, "Very well, you can come at this time tomorrow for your first lesson."

The young deer came to the lessons as he was supposed to. When others cut classes to spend all day playing, he remained and paid attention to the good teacher. He was well liked by the other young bucks and does, but he only played when his class work was complete. Being curious to learn, he was always on time for the lessons. He was also patient with the other students, knowing that some learn more quickly than others. He respected the teacher deer for his knowledge, and was grateful for his willingness to share it.

One day, the fawn stepped in a trap in the forest and was captured. He cried out in great pain. This frightened the other fawns, who ran back to the herd and told his mother. She was terrified, and ran to her brother the teacher. Trembling with fear, crying big tears, she said to him, "Oh my dear brother, have you heard the news that my son has been trapped by some hunter's snare? How can I save my little child's life? Did he study well in your presence?"

Her brother said, "My sister, don't be afraid. I have no doubt he will be safe. He studied hard and always did his very best. He never missed a class and always paid attention. Therefore, there is no need to have doubt or pain in your heart. He will not be hurt by any human being. Don't worry. I am confident he will return to you and make you happy again. He has learned all the tricks and strategies used by deer to cheat the hunters. So be patient. He will return!"

Meanwhile, the trapped fawn was thinking, "All my friends were afraid and ran away. There is no one to help me get out of this deadly trap. Now I must use the tricks and strategies I learned from the wise teacher who taught so well."

The deer strategy he decided to use was the one called, "playing dead." First, he used his hoofs to dig up the dirt and grass, to make it look like he had tried very hard to escape. Then he relieved his bowels and released his urine, because this is what happens when a deer is caught in a trap and dies in very great fear. Next, he covered his body with his own saliva.

Lying stretched out on his side, he held his body rigidly and stiffened his legs out straight. He turned up his eyes, and let his tongue hang out of the side of his mouth. He filled his lungs with air and puffed out his belly. Finally, with his head leaning on one side, he breathed through the nostril next to the ground, not through the upper one.

Lying motionless, he looked so much like a stiff corpse that flies flew around him, attracted by the awful smells. Crows stood nearby waiting to eat his flesh.

Before long it was early morning and the hunter came to inspect his traps. Finding the fawn who was playing dead, he slapped the puffed-up belly and found it stiff. Seeing the flies and the mess he thought, "Ah, it has already started to stiffen. He must have been trapped much earlier this morning. No doubt the tender meat is already starting to spoil. I will skin and butcher the carcass right here, and carry the meat home."

Since he completely believed the deer was dead, he removed and cleaned the trap, and began spreading leaves to make a place to do the butchering. Realizing he was free, the fawn suddenly sprang to his feet.

He ran like a little cloud blown by a swift wind, back to the comfort and safety of his mother. The whole herd celebrated his survival, thanks to learning so well from the wise teacher.

The Buddha then connected the births in this way:

"The obedient fawn Rāhula was the present Rāhula. His mother was the nun Uppalavaṇṇā. And I who am today the Buddha was the deer who was the teacher."

The moral: "Well-learned lessons bring great rewards."

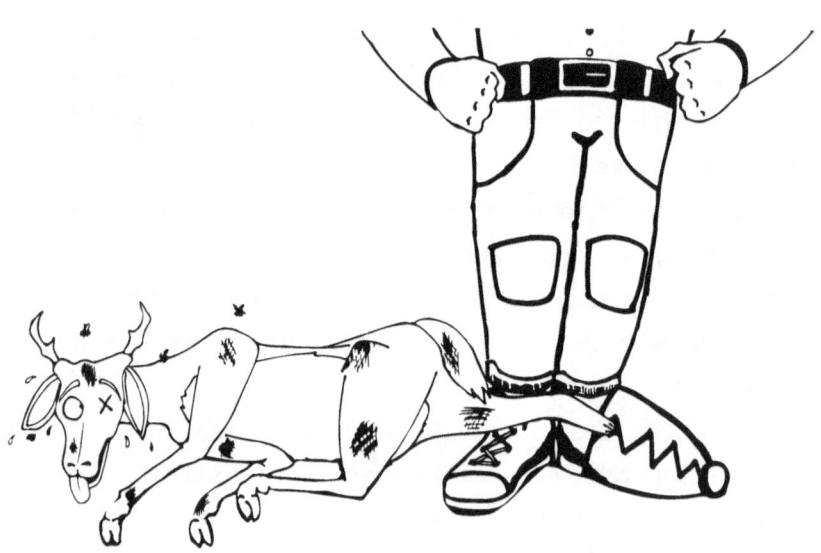

17

The Wind and the Moon
[Friendship]
(*Māluta-Jātaka*)

W hen the Buddha was living in Jetavana monastery at Sāvatthi, he told this story on account of two monks who had been ordained when they were old, and who lived in a hermitage in the forest. One was named Juṇha, and the other was named Kāla.[13] One day, Juṇha asked Kāla, "When does it get cold?" Kāla said, "It will get cold in the dark half of the month." Then, on another day, Kāla asked Juṇha, "When does it get cold?" And Juṇha said, "It will get cold in the light half of the month."

They were now in a difficult situation. They could not decide when it would get cold. Was it when it would be dark, or when it would be light? As they could not solve the question, they went to see the Buddha.

When the Buddha heard what they said, he said, "Oh monks, I helped you solve this question even in the past. But as your previous re-becomings have been obscured by time, you do not remember the answer." And saying this, the Buddha told them this story of the past:

Once upon a time, there were two very good friends who lived together in the shade of a rock. Strange as it may seem, one was a lion and one was a tiger. They had met when they were too young to know the difference between lions and tigers. So they did not think their friendship was at all unusual. Besides, it was a peaceful part of the mountains, possibly due to the influence of a gentle forest monk who lived nearby. He was a hermit, one who lives far away from other people.

---

13 The name Juṇha refers to the bright fortnight of a lunar month, or moonlight. The name Kāla refers to darkness, or the dark fortnight of the moon.

For some unknown reason, one day the two friends got into a silly argument. The tiger said, "Everyone knows the cold comes when the moon wanes from full to new!" The lion said, "Where did you hear such nonsense? Everyone knows the cold comes when the moon waxes from new to full!"

The argument got stronger and stronger. Neither could convince the other. They could not reach any conclusion to resolve the growing dispute. They even started calling each other names! Fearing for their friendship, they decided to go ask the learned forest monk who, as it happened, was the Enlightenment Being, who would surely know about such things.

Visiting the peaceful hermit, the lion and tiger bowed respectfully and put their question to him. The friendly monk thought for a while and then gave his answer. "It can be cold in any phase of the moon, from new to full and back to new again. It is the wind that brings the cold, whether from west or north or east. Therefore, in a way, you are both right! And neither of you is defeated by the other. The most important thing is to live without conflict, to remain united. Unity is best by all means."

The lion and tiger thanked the wise hermit. They were happy to still be friends.

The Buddha then said, "Oh monks, in this way I solved this question in the past." And the Buddha then pointed out the Four Noble Truths [*cattāri ariya-saccāni*], that life is by nature full of sorrow, the cause of sorrow is craving, it can only be stopped by stopping craving, this can only be done by practicing disciplined and moral conduct culminating in the life of concentration and meditation of a Buddhist monk. After the explanation of the Four Noble Truths, the two monks attained the stream entrance state of mind [*sotāpatti*].

The Buddha then ended by saying:

"The tiger at that time was Kāla, and the lion was Juṇha. The ascetic who solved the dispute was I who have become the fully enlightened one."

The moral: "Weather comes and weather goes, but friendship remains."

18

The Goat Who Saved the Priest
[Ignorance]
(Matakabhatta-Jātaka)

When the Buddha was living in Jetavana monastery, he told this story with reference to the feast for dead ancestors. At that time, in the city of Sāvatthi, every year the people performed a certain ceremony in which there was a sacrifice of many animals. The merit from this was given to their departed relatives who had died in old age.

Some monks, seeing people going to the sacrificial grounds, asked these people why they were going there. And the people told them why. The monks then went to the Buddha and asked, "Venerable sir, the people of Sāvatthi are at present killing hundreds of living beings in a feast for dead ancestors. Is there any advantage to such an activity?" The Buddha said, "Oh monks, by killing these innocent living beings there is not the least bit of advantage. Even in the past, I admonished against such killing, and it was stopped. But it has reappeared on account of the curtain created by many re-becomings."

The monks then asked the Buddha to disclose the past story. And the Buddha disclosed the story in this way:

Once upon a time, there was a very famous priest in a very old religion. He decided it was the right day to perform the ritual sacrificing of a goat. In his ignorance, he thought this was an offering demanded by his god.

He obtained an appropriate goat for the sacrifice. He ordered his servants to take the goat to the holy river and wash him and decorate him with flower garlands. Then they were to wash themselves, as part of the purification practice.

Down at the riverbank, the goat suddenly understood that today he would definitely be killed. He also became aware of his past births and deaths and rebirths. He realized that the results of his past unwholesome deeds were about to finally be completed. So he laughed an uproarious goat-laugh, like the clanging of cymbals.

In the midst of his laughter, he realized another truth – that the priest, by sacrificing him, would suffer the same terrible results, due to his ignorance. So he began to cry as loudly as he had just been laughing!

The servants, who were bathing in the holy river, heard first the laughing and then the crying. They were amazed. So they asked the goat, "Why did you loudly laugh and then just as loudly cry? What is the reason for this?" He replied, "I will tell you the reason. But it must be in the presence of your master, the priest."

Since they were very curious, they immediately took the sacrificial goat to the priest. They explained all that had happened. The priest too, became very curious. He respectfully asked the goat, "Sir, why did you laugh so loudly, and then just as loudly cry?"

The goat, remembering his past lives, said, "A long time ago, I too was a priest who, like you, was well educated in the sacred religious rites. I thought that to sacrifice a goat was a necessary offering to my god, which would benefit others, as well as myself in future rebirths. However, the true result of my action was that in my next 499 lives I myself have been beheaded!

"While being prepared for the sacrifice, I realized that today I will definitely lose my head for the 500th time. Then I will finally be free of all the results of my unwholesome deed of so long ago. The joy of this made me laugh uncontrollably.

"Then I suddenly realized that you, the priest, were about to repeat the same unwholesome action, and would be doomed to the same result of having your head chopped off in your next 500 lives! So, out of compassion and sympathy, my laughter turned to tears."

The priest was afraid this goat might be right, so he said, "Well, sir goat, I will not kill you." The goat replied, "Reverend priest, even if you do not kill me, I know that today I will lose my head and finally be released from the results of my past unwholesome action."

The priest said, "Don't be afraid, my fine goat. I will provide the very best protection and personally guarantee that no harm will come to you." But the goat said, "Oh priest, your protection is very weak, compared to the power of my unwholesome deed to cause its necessary results."

So the priest canceled the sacrifice, and began to have doubts about killing innocent animals. He released the goat and, along with his servants, followed him in order to protect him from any danger.

The goat wandered into a rocky place. He saw some tender leaves on a branch and stretched out his neck to reach them. All of a sudden a thunderstorm appeared out of nowhere. A lightning bolt struck an overhanging rock, and cut off a sharp slab, which fell and chopped off the goat's head! He died instantly, and the thunderstorm disappeared.

Hearing of this very strange event, hundreds of local people came to the place. No one could understand how it had happened.

There was also a fairy who lived in a nearby tree. He had seen all that had occurred. He appeared, gently fluttering in the air overhead. He began to teach the curious people, saying, "Look at what happened to this poor goat. This was the result of killing animals! All beings are born, and suffer through sickness, old age and death. But all wish to live, and not to die. Not seeing that all have this in common, some kill other living beings.

This causes suffering also to those who kill, both now and in countless future rebirths.

"Being ignorant that all deeds must cause results to the doer, some continue to kill and heap up more suffering on themselves in the future. Each time they kill, a part of themselves must also die in this present life. And the suffering continues even by rebirth in hell worlds!"

Those who heard the fairy speak felt that they were very lucky indeed. They gave up their ignorant killing, and were far better off, both in this life and in pleasant rebirths.

The Buddha then said:

"The tree fairy was I who have become the Buddha."

The moral: "Even religion can be a source of ignorance."

$$\boxed{19}$$

The God in the Banyan Tree
[A Bad Promise]
(*Āyācitabhatta-Jātaka, Pāṇavadha-Jātaka*)

When the Buddha was living in Jetavana temple, he told this story about a sacrificial vow that was being made to gods at that time. Before people went on a journey to sell their goods, they would sacrifice living creatures to gods. They thought their venture would be successful because of their sacrifice. And they would make a vow that if their venture turned out well, when they would come back, they would perform even more sacrifices.

About this, some monks asked the Buddha, "Bhante, is there any advantage on account of such sacrifices?" The Buddha then said, "The answer to this has been clouded over by many re-becomings." And the Buddha told this story of the past:

In the past, and even in some places today, people have had superstitions. One such is that a large or unusual tree is inhabited by a tree god, or some kind of spirit. People think that they can make a promise to this tree god, so he will help them in some way. When they think the god has helped them, then they must keep their promise.

Once upon a time, in the city of Kāsi[14] in northern India, a man came upon a large banyan tree. He immediately thought there must be a god living there. So he made a promise to this tree god that he would perform an animal sacrifice in return for a wish being granted.

It just so happened that his wish was fulfilled, but whether by a god or a demon or by some other means – no one knows. The man

_____
14 Kāsi was a suburb of Benares at this time.

was sure the tree god had answered his prayer, so he wanted to keep his promise.

Since it was a big wish, it called for a big sacrifice. He brought many goats, mules, chickens and sheep. He collected firewood and prepared to burn the helpless animals as a sacrifice.

The spirit living in the banyan tree appeared and said, "Oh friend, you made a promise. You are now bound by that promise. You think you must keep the promise in order to be released from the bondage to it. But if you commit such terrible unwholesome acts, even though promised, the unpleasant results will put you in much greater bondage. For you will be forced to suffer those results in this life, and even by rebirths in hell worlds! The way to release yourself into future deliverance is to give up unwholesome actions, no matter what!

"And furthermore, since you think I'm a true god, what makes you think I eat meat? Haven't you heard that we gods eat better things, like

'ambrosia' or stardust or sunbeams? I have no need of meat or any other food offerings." Then he disappeared.

The foolish man understood the mistake he had made. Instead of doing unwholesome deeds that would force unhappy results on him in the future, he began to do only wholesome deeds that would benefit himself and others.

The Buddha then ended this Jātaka story by saying:

"The god living in the banyan tree was I who am today the Buddha."

The moral: "Keeping a bad promise is worse than making it."

20

The Monkey King and the Water Demon
[Attentiveness]
(Naḷapāna-Jātaka)

The Buddha told this story while he was on an alms pilgrimage when he had come to the village of Naḷakapāna and was dwelling in Ketaka Forest [Ketaka-vana][15] near the Naḷakapāna Pond, about cane straws made from a small kind of bamboo. At that time, the monks with the Buddha bathed in the pond, and took cane sticks for needle cases. But they found that the cane sticks were hollow throughout. They then went to the Buddha and said, "Venerable sir, we took cane sticks from the pond to make needle cases; but they are hollow from top to bottom. How can that be?"

The Buddha then said, "Oh monks, this is on account of an order of mine in a previous birth." And saying this, he told this story of the past:

Once upon a time, far away in a deep forest, there was a nation of 80,000 monkeys. They had a king who was unusually large, as big as a fawn. He was not only big in body, he was also 'large in mind'. After all, he was the Bodhisatta – the Enlightenment Being.

One day, he advised his monkey nation by saying, "My subjects, there are poisonous fruits in this deep forest, and ponds possessed by demons. So if you see any unusual fruit or unknown pond, do not eat or drink until you ask me first." Paying close attention to their wise king, all the monkeys agreed to follow his advice.

Later on, they came to an unknown pond. Even though they were all tired out and thirsty from searching for food, no one would drink without first asking the monkey king. So they sat in the trees and on the ground around the pond.

---

15 Ketaka is a very fragrant flower used to make mats.

When he arrived, the monkey king asked them, "Did anyone drink the water?" They replied, "No, your majesty, we followed your instructions." He said, "Well done."

Then he walked along the bank, around the pond. He examined the footprints of the animals that had gone into the water, and saw that none came out again! So he realized this pond must be possessed by a water demon. He said to the 80,000 monkeys, "This pond is possessed by a water demon. Do not anybody go into it."

After a little while, the water demon saw that none of the monkeys went into the water to drink. So he rose out of the middle of the pond, taking the shape of a frightening monster. He had a big blue belly, a white face with bulging green eyes, and red claws and feet. He said, "Why are you just sitting around? Come into the pond and drink at once!"

The monkey king said to the horrible monster, "Are you the water demon who owns this pond?" "Yes, I am," said he. "Do you eat whoever goes into the water?" asked the king. "Yes, I do," he answered, "including even birds. I eat them all. And when you are forced by your thirst to come into the pond and drink, I will enjoy eating you, the biggest monkey, most of all!" He grinned, and saliva dripped down his hairy chin.

But the monkey king with the well-trained mind remained calm. He said, "I will not let you eat me or a single one of my followers. And yet, we will drink all the water we want!" The water demon grunted, "Impossible! How will you do that?" The monkey king replied, "Each one of the 80,000 of us will drink using bamboo shoots as straws. And you will not be able to touch us!"

Of course, anyone who has seen bamboo knows there is a difficulty. Bamboo grows in sections, one after another, with a knot between each one. Any one section is too small, so the demon could grab the monkey, pull him under and gobble him up. But the knots make it impossible to sip through more than one section.

The monkey king was very special, and that is why so many followed him. In the past, he had practiced goodness and trained his mind with such effort and attention, that he had developed very fine qualities of mind. This is why he was said to be 'large in mind', not because he simply had a 'big brain'.

The Enlightenment Being was able to keep these fine qualities in his mind, and produce a very unlikely event – a miracle. First, he took a young bamboo shoot, blew through it to make the knots disappear, and used it to sip water from the pond. Then, amazing as it may sound, he waved his hand and all the bamboo growing around that one pond lost their knots. They became a new kind of bamboo.

Then, all his 80,000 followers picked bamboo shoots and easily drank their fill from the pond. The water demon could not believe his green eyes. Grumbling to himself, he slid back under the surface, leaving only gurgling bubbles behind.

When the Buddha had ended his story, he said:

"The water demon at that time was Devadatta. The 80,000 monkeys are today my disciples. And the clever monkey king who was resourceful enough to save the lives of the 80,000 monkeys was I who am today the Buddha."

The moral:
"Test the water before jumping in."

21

The Tree That Acted Like a Hunter
[Impatience]
(Kuruṅga-Jātaka)

This story was told by the Buddha while he was living in the Bamboo Grove temple with regard to Devadatta.

At one time, the monks assembled in the preaching hall in the evening were discussing with reproach Devadatta's attempts to kill the Buddha. They said, "Devadatta is trying to kill the Buddha by hiring bowmen to shoot him, hurling a rock at him and letting loose the elephant Dhanapālaka[16] in his path. In every way, he is trying to kill the Buddha." When the Buddha entered the hall, he asked the monks, "Oh monks, what were you talking about before I came here?" The monks replied, "Venerable sir, we were discussing Devadatta's criminal acts trying to kill you, but always failing to do so." The Buddha said, "Oh monks, it is not only today that Devadatta goes about trying to kill me. He did so also in the past, but just so was unable to kill me." And the Buddha then told this story of the past:

Once upon a time, there was an antelope who lived in the deep forest. He ate the fruits that fell from the trees. There was one Sepaṇṇi-tree[17] that had become his favorite.

In the same area there was a hunter who captured and killed antelopes and deer. He put down fruit as bait under a tree. Then he waited, hiding in the branches above. He held a rope noose hanging down to the ground around the fruits. When an animal ate the fruit, the hunter tightened the noose and caught him.

16 Elsewhere, the elephant is called Nālāgiri.
17 Literally, 'having lucky leaves'; the tree Gmelina arborea.

Early one morning the antelope came to his favorite tree in search of fruits to eat. He did not see that the hunter was hiding in it, with his noose trap ready. Even though he was hungry, the antelope was very careful. He was on the lookout for any possible danger. He saw the delicious looking ripe fruits at the foot of his favorite tree. He wondered why no animal had yet eaten any, and so he was afraid something was wrong.

The hiding hunter saw the antelope approaching from a distance. Seeing him stop and take great care, he was afraid he would not be able to trap him. He was so anxious that he began throwing fruits in the direction of the antelope, trying to lure him into coming closer.

But this was a pretty smart antelope. He knew that fruits only fall straight down when they fall from trees. Since these fruits were flying towards him, he knew there was danger. So he examined the tree itself very carefully, and saw the hunter in the branches. However, he pretended not to see him.

He spoke in the direction of the tree. "Oh, my dear fruit tree, you used to give me your fruits by letting them fall straight down to the ground. Now, throwing them towards me, you do not act at all like a tree! Since you have changed your habits, I too will change mine. I will get my fruits from a different tree from now on, one that still acts like a tree!"

The hunter realized his mistake and saw that the antelope had outsmarted him. This angered him and he yelled out, "You may escape me this time, you clever antelope, but I'll get you next time for sure!"

The antelope realized that, by getting so angry, the hunter had given himself away a second time. So he spoke in the direction of the tree again. "Not only don't you act like a tree, but you act like a hunter! You foolish humans, who live by killing animals. You do not understand that killing the innocent brings harm also to you, both in this life and by rebirth in a hell world. It is clear that we antelopes are far wiser than you. We eat fruits, we remain innocent of killing others, and we avoid the harmful results."

So saying, the careful antelope leaped into the thick forest and was gone.

When the Buddha ended this Jātaka story and had told the monks present about Devadatta's trying to kill but failing to do it in the past, he said:

"The hunter in those days was Devadatta, and the antelope was I myself who have become the Buddha."

The moral: "The wise remain innocent."

22

The Dog King Silver
[Justice]
(Kukkura-Jātaka)

This story was told by the Buddha while he was living in Jetavana monastery about acting for the benefit of relatives, as will be related in the twelfth book in the *Baddasāla-Jātaka* [No. 465].

[While the Buddha was living in Jetavana monastery, King Pasenadi of Kosala wanted to give alms to the monks. But on that day, there was not even a single monk in the monastery. The king thought, "I always give alms. But the monks do not have full confidence in me because I am not a relative of the Buddha. If I became a relative, the monks would be more confident in and friendly to me." Therefore, he sent a message to the Sakyā king requesting him to give a Sakyā virgin princess as his queen. So the Sakyā king, who was afraid of the king of Kosala because he was mighty and powerful, thought, "It is good to give a girl to him. But we ought not give him a real Sakyā girl. We will give him a half Sakyā girl." Thinking so, he gave him the princess Vāsabhakkhattiyā, who was the daughter of the Sakyā Mahānāma by a slave girl.

After Vāsabhakkhattiyā had given birth to a son for him, named Viḍūḍabha, King Pasenadi eventually came to understand what had happened. At that time, he cut off Vāsabhakkhattiyā's and Viḍūḍabha's royal allowances, and he treated them as he would treat slaves. Buddha interceded, and he convinced him to reinstate Vāsabhakkhattiyā and Viḍūḍabha to their noble status.[18]

---

18 See Jātaka No. 7, the *Kaṭṭhahāri-Jātaka*, above.

Eventually Viḍūḍabha, after he had become king of Kosala, as he harbored resentment toward the Sakyā-s for their insult to his father, attacked the Sakyā-s at Kapilavatthu. On the way, three times the Buddha met him and persuaded him not to attack. On the fourth time, the Buddha understood that because of the Sakyā-s' previous deeds (Kamma), he could not prevent the attack. At that time, Viḍūḍabha destroyed all the Sakyā families.

This news spread even among the monks. They were discussing it one day in the preaching hall, saying that the Buddha had not been able to prevent the killing of the

Sakyā-s because of their Kamma, even though he had tried to intercede three times. Three times, though, the Buddha turned back Viḍūḍabha. Fully three times the Buddha tried to save his relatives from danger. Buddha is, indeed, a helpful friend to his kin.]

It was to drive home this lesson that the Buddha told this story of the past.

Once upon time, the King of Benares went to his pleasure garden in his fancy decorated chariot. He loved this chariot, mostly because of the rich hand-worked leather belts and straps.

On this occasion, he stayed in his pleasure garden all day long and into the evening. It was late when he finally got back to the palace. So the chariot was left outside in the compound all night, instead of being locked up properly.

During the night it rained heavily, and the leather got wet, swelled up, became soft, and gave off an odor. The pampered palace dogs smelled the delicious leather scent and came down into the compound. They chewed off and devoured the soft wet chariot straps. Before daybreak, they returned unseen to their places in the palace.

When the king woke up and came down, he saw that the leather had been chewed off and eaten by dogs. He called the servants and demanded to know how this happened.

Since they were supposed to watch the palace dogs, the servants were afraid to blame them. Instead, they made up a story that stray dogs, the mutts and mongrels of the city, had come into the grounds through sewers and storm drains. They were the ones who had eaten the fancy leather.

The king flew into a terrible rage. He was so overcome by anger that he decided to take vengeance against all dogs. So he decreed that whenever anyone in the city saw a dog, he was to kill him or her at once!

The people began killing dogs. The dogs could not understand why suddenly they were being killed. Later that day, they learned of the king's decree. They became very frightened and retreated to the cemetery just outside the city. This was where their leader lived, the Dog King Silver [Rajata].

Silver was king not because he was the biggest or strongest or toughest. He was average in size, with sleek silver fur, sparkling black eyes and alert pointed ears. He walked with great dignity, which brought admiration and respect from men as well as dogs. In his long life he had learned much, and was able to concentrate his mind on what is most important. So he became the wisest of all the dogs, as well as the one who cared most for the others. Those were the reasons he was king of the dogs.

In the cemetery, the dogs were in a panic. They were frightened to death. The Dog King Silver asked them why this was. They told him all about the chariot straps and the king's decree, and the people killing them whenever they saw them.

King Silver knew there was no way to get into the well guarded palace grounds. So he understood that the leather must have been eaten by the dogs living inside the palace.

He thought, "We dogs know that, no matter how different we may appear, somehow we are all related. So now I must make my greatest effort to save the lives of all these poor dogs, my relatives. There is no one to save them but me."

He comforted them by saying, "Do not be afraid. I will save you all. Stay here in the cemetery and don't go into the city. I will tell the King of Benares who are the thieves and who are the innocent. The truth will save us all."

Before setting out, he went to a different part of the cemetery to be alone. Having practiced goodness all his life, and trained his mind, he now concentrated very hard and filled his mind with feelings of loving-kindness [*mettā*]. He thought, "May all dogs be well and happy, and may all dogs be safe. I go to the palace for the sake of dogs and men alike. No one shall attack or harm me."

Then the Dog King Silver began walking slowly through the streets of Benares. Because his mind was focused, he had no fear. Because of his long life of goodness, he walked with a calm dignity that demanded respect. And because of the warm glow of loving-kindness that all the people sensed, no one felt the rising of anger or any intention to harm him. Instead, they marveled as the Great Being [Bodhisatta] passed, and wondered how it could be so!

It was as if the whole city were entranced. With no obstruction, the Dog King Silver walked right past the palace guards, into the royal hall of justice, and sat down calmly underneath the king's throne itself! The King of Benares was impressed by such courage and dignity. So when servants came to remove the dog, he ordered them to let him remain.

Then the Dog King Silver came out from under the throne and faced the mighty King of Benares. He bowed respectfully and asked, "Your majesty, was it you who ordered that all the dogs of the city should be killed?" "It was I," replied the king. "What crime did the dogs commit?" asked the dog king. "Dogs ate my rich beautiful chariot leather and straps." "Do you know which dogs did this?" asked King Silver. "No one knows," said the King of Benares.

"My lord," said the dog, "for a king such as you, who wishes to be righteous, is it right to have all dogs killed in the place of the few guilty ones? Does this do justice to the innocent ones?" The king replied, as if it made perfect sense to him, "Since I do not know which dogs destroyed my leather, only by ordering the killing of all dogs can I be sure of punishing the guilty. The king must have justice!"

The Dog King Silver paused for a moment, before challenging the king with the crucial question – "My lord king, is it a fact that you have ordered all dogs to be killed, or are there some who are not to be killed?" The king suddenly became a little uneasy as he was forced to admit, before his whole court, "It is true that most dogs are to be killed, but not all. The fine pure-breeds of my palace are to be spared."

Then the dog king said, "My lord, before you said that all dogs were to be killed, in order to ensure that the guilty would be punished. Now you say that your own palace dogs are to be spared. This shows that you have gone wrong in the way of prejudice. For a king who wishes to be righteous, it is wrong to favor some over others. The king's justice must be unbiased, like an honest scale. Although you have decreed an impartial death to all dogs, in fact this is only the slaughter of poor dogs. Your rich palace dogs are unjustly saved, while the poor are wrongly killed!"

Recognizing the truth of the dog king's words, the King of Benares asked, "Are you wise enough to know which dogs ate my leather straps and belts?" "Yes my lord, I do know," said he, "it could only be your own favorite palace dogs, and I can prove it." "Do so," said the king.

The dog king asked to have the palace pets brought into the hall of justice. He asked for a mixture of buttermilk and grass, and for the dogs to be made to eat it. Lo and behold, when this was done they vomited up partly digested pieces of the king's leather straps!

Then the Dog King Silver said, "My lord, no poor dogs from the city can enter the well guarded palace compound. You were blinded by prejudice. It is your dogs who are the guilty ones. Nevertheless, to kill any living being is an unwholesome thing to do. This is because of what we dogs know, but men do not seem to know – that somehow all life is related, so all living beings deserve the same respect as relatives."

The whole court was amazed by what had just taken place. The King of Benares was suddenly overcome by a rare feeling of humility. He bowed before the dog king and said, "Oh great king of dogs, I have never

seen anyone such as you, one who combines perfect wisdom with great compassion. Truly, your justice is supreme. I offer my throne and the kingdom of Benares to you!"

The Enlightenment Being replied, "Arise my lord, I have no desire for a human crown. If you wish to show your respect for me, you should be a just and merciful ruler.[19] It would help if you begin to purify your mind by practicing the 'Five Training Steps' [*pañca-sīla*-s, the first five *sikkhā-pada*-s]. These are to give up entirely the five unwholesome actions: destroying life, taking what is not given, sexual wrong-doing, speaking falsely, and drunkenness."

The king followed the teachings of the wise dog king. He ruled with great respect for all living beings. He ordered that whenever he ate, all

---

19 At this point, the Enlightenment Being recites the ten stanzas on the ways of righteousness found in the *Tesakuṇa-Jātaka* [No. 521].

dogs, those of the palace and those of the city, were to be fed as well. This was the beginning of the faithfulness between dogs and men that has lasted to this day.

When the Buddha ended this Jātaka story, he said, "Not only today, even in the past I helped my relatives."

The Buddha then connected the births, saying:

"The king at that time was the Venerable Ānanda. The dogs in the cemetery who were related to the Dog King Silver are today my followers and relatives. And I myself who have become the Buddha was the Dog King Silver."

The moral: "One should always help one's relatives."

Also, "Prejudice leads to injustice. Wisdom leads to justice."

The Great Horse Knowing-one[20]
[Courage]
(Bhojājānīya-Jātaka)

The Buddha told this story while he was living in Jetavana monastery with regard to a monk who had given up striving to meditate for the purpose of understanding the teachings of the Buddha. When the Buddha heard about this, he asked that monk, "Oh monk, is it true that you have given up your striving to meditate?" The monk answered, "Yes, Venerable sir, it is so." The Buddha then said, "Oh monk, it is not good to give up your perseverance on meditation." And the Buddha told this story:

* * *

(Ājañña-Jātaka)

The Buddha told this story while he was living in Jetavana monastery with regard to another monk who had given up persevering.

* * *

Once upon a time, King Brahmadatta ruled in Benares, in northern India. He had a mighty horse who had been born in the land of Sindh in the Indus River valley of western India. Indeed, this horse was the Enlightenment Being.

As well as being big and strong, he was very intelligent and wise. When he was still young, people noticed that he always seemed to know what his rider wanted before being told. So he was called Knowing-one.

He was considered the greatest of the royal horses, and was given

---

20 An *ājānīya*, or *ājañña* horse knows what its rider wants it to do intuitively.

the very best of everything. His stall was decorated and was always kept clean and beautiful. Horses are usually faithful to their masters. Knowing-one was especially loyal, and was grateful for how well the king cared for him. Of all the royal horses, Knowing-one was also the bravest. So the king respected and trusted him.

It came to pass that seven neighboring kings joined together to make war on King Brahmadatta. Each king brought four great armies – an elephant cavalry, a horse cavalry, a chariot brigade and ranks of foot soldiers. Together the seven kings, with all their armies, surrounded the city of Benares.

King Brahmadatta assembled his ministers and advisers to make plans for defending the kingdom. They advised him, "Do not surrender. We must fight to protect our high positions. But you should not risk your royal person in the beginning. Instead, send out the champion of all the knights to represent you on the battlefield. If he fails, only then must you yourself go."

So the king called the champion to him and asked, "Can you be victorious over these seven kings?" The knight replied, "If you permit me to ride out on the bravest and wisest, the great horse Knowing-one, only then can I win the battle." The king agreed and said, "My champion, it is up to you and Knowing-one to save the country in its time of danger. Take with you whatever you need."

The champion knight went to the royal stables. He ordered that Knowing-one be well fed and dressed in protective armor, with all the finest trimmings. Then he bowed respectfully and climbed into the beautiful saddle.

Knowing-one knew the situation. He thought, "These seven kings have come to attack my country and my king, who feeds and cares for and trusts me. Not only the seven kings, but also their large and powerful armies threaten my king and all in Benares. I cannot let them win. But I also cannot permit the champion knight to kill those kings. Then I too would share in the unwholesome action of taking the lives of others, in order to win an ordinary victory. Instead, I will teach a new way. I will capture all seven kings without killing anyone. That would be a truly great victory!"

Then the Knowing-one spoke to his rider. "Sir knight, let us win this battle in a new way, without destroying life. You must only capture each king, one at a time, and remain firmly on my back. Let me find the true course through the many armies. Watch me as you ride, and I will show you the courage that goes beyond the old way, the killing way!"

As he spoke of 'a new way', and 'the true course', and 'the courage that goes beyond', it seemed the noble steed became larger than life. He reared up majestically on his powerful hind legs, and looked down on all the armies surrounding the city. The eyes of all were drawn to this magnificent one. The earth trembled as his front hoofs returned to the ground and he charged into the midst of the four armies of the first king. He seemed to have the speed of lightning, the might of a hundred elephants, and the glorious confidence of one from some other world.

The elephants could remember no such horse as this, and so the elephant cavalry retreated in fear. The horses knew that this their relative was the worthy master of them all, and so the horse cavalry and the chariot brigade stood still and bowed as the Great Being [Bodhisatta] passed. And

the ranks of foot soldiers scattered like flies before a strong wind.

The first king hardly knew what had happened, before he was easily captured and brought back into the city of Benares. And so too with the second, third, fourth and fifth kings.

In the same way the sixth king was captured. But one of his loyal bodyguards leaped out from hiding and thrust his sword deep into the side of the brave Knowing-one. With blood streaming from the wound, he carried the champion knight and the captured sixth king back to the city.

When the knight saw the terrible wound, he suddenly became afraid to ride the weakened Knowing-one against the seventh king. So he began to dress in armor another powerful war horse, who was really just as big as Knowing-one.

Seeing this, though suffering in great pain from his deadly wound, Knowing-one thought, "This champion knight has lost his courage so quickly. He has not understood the true nature of my power – the knowledge that true peace is only won by peaceful means. He tries to defeat the seventh king and his armies in the ordinary way, riding an ordinary horse.

"After taking the first step of giving up the killing of living beings, I cannot stop part way. My great effort to teach a new way would disappear like a line drawn in water!"

The great horse Knowing-one spoke to the champion knight. "Sir knight, the seventh king and his armies are the mightiest of all. Riding an ordinary horse, even if you slaughter a thousand men and animals, you will be defeated. I, of the mighty tribe of Sindh horses, the one called Knowing-one, only I can pass through them harming none, and bring back the seventh king alive!"

The champion knight regained his courage. The brave horse struggled to his feet, in great pain. While the blood continued to flow, he reared and charged through the four armies, and the knight brought back the last of the seven warlike kings. Again all those in his path were spared from harm. Seeing their seven kings in captivity, all the armies laid down their weapons and asked for peace.

Realizing that the great horse Knowing-one would not live through the night, King Brahmadatta went to see him. He had raised him from a colt, so he loved him. When he saw that he was dying, his eyes filled with tears.

Knowing-one said, "My lord king, I have served you well. And I have gone beyond and shown a new way. Now you must grant my last request. You must not kill these seven kings, even though they have wronged you. For, a bloody victory sews the seeds of the next war. Forgive their attack on you, let them return to their kingdoms, and may you all live in peace from now on.

"Whatever reward you would give to me, give instead to the champion knight. Do only wholesome deeds, be generous, honor the Truth [Dhamma], and kill no living being. Rule with justice and compassion."

Then he closed his eyes and breathed his last. The king burst into tears, and all mourned his passing. With the highest honors, they burned the body of the great horse Knowing-one – the Enlightenment Being.

King Brahmadatta had the seven kings brought before him. They too honored the great one, who had defeated their vast armies without spilling a drop of blood, except his own. In his memory they made peace, and never again did these seven kings and Brahmadatta make war on each other.

* * *

23. "At that time, the king was the Venerable Ānanda. The knight was the Venerable Sāriputta. And I myself who have become the Buddha was the noble horse."

* * *

24. "At that time, the king was the Venerable Ānanda. And I who am the Buddha was the horse who persevered and captured the seventh king."

The moral: "Great effort brings great results."

Also, "True peace is only won by peaceful means."

25

Dirty Bath Water
[Cleanliness]
(Tittha-Jātaka)

This story was told by the Buddha while he was dwelling at Jetavana monastery about a monk who was a disciple of the Venerable Sāriputta and who before becoming a monk had been a goldsmith.

This monk meditated for many months, but without any successful results. On account of this, he was summoned by the Venerable Sāriputta and taken to the Buddha. Sāriputta explained the situation to the Buddha and leaving this monk with the Buddha, he went back to his own monastery.

Buddha gave this monk food to eat, and creating the illusion of a beautiful lotus in a pond, told the monk to meditate on it. While this monk was meditating, the lotus became old, and its petals fell. And the monk gained insight from this, and attained Arahant-ship [sainthood].

This became known to the Buddha and the Venerable Sāriputta, and to the other monks.

One day, the monks were discussing this in the preaching hall when the Buddha entered. The Buddha explained that a similar incident had occurred in Benares in the past with regard to this same monk. And the monks present asked the Buddha to tell the story.

This is how it was:

Once upon a time, in a kingdom in India, the finest of the royal horses was taken down to the river to be bathed. The grooms took him to the same shallow pool where they always washed him.

However, just before they arrived, a filthy dirty horse had been washed in the same spot. He had been caught in the countryside and had never had a good bath in all his life.

The fine royal horse sniffed the air. He knew right away that some filthy wild horse had bathed there and fouled the water. So he was disgusted and refused to be washed at that place.

The grooms tried their best to get him into the water, but could do nothing with him. So they went to the king and complained that the fine well trained royal stallion had suddenly become stubborn and unmanageable.

It just so happened that the king had an intelligent minister who was known for his understanding of animals. So he called for him and said, "Please go and see what has happened to my number one horse. Find out if he is sick or what is the reason he refuses to be bathed. Of all my horses, I thought this one was of such high quality that he would never let himself sink into dirtiness. There must be something wrong."

The minister went down to the riverside bathing pool immediately. He found that the stately horse was not sick, but in perfect health. He noticed also that he was deliberately breathing as little as possible. So he sniffed the air and smelled a slight foul odor. Investigating further, he found that it came from the unclean water in the bathing pool. So he figured out that another very dirty horse must have been washed there, and that the king's horse was too fond of cleanliness to bathe in dirty water.

The minister asked the horse grooms, "Has any other horse been bathed at this spot today?" "Yes," they replied, "before we arrived, a dirty wild horse was bathed here." The minister told them, "My dear grooms, this is a fine royal horse who loves cleanliness. He does not wish to bathe in dirty water. So the thing to do is to take him up river, where the water is fresh and clean, and wash him there."

They followed his instructions, and the royal horse was pleased to bathe in the new place.

The minister returned to the king and told what had happened. Then he said, "You were correct your majesty, this fine horse was indeed of such high quality that he would not let himself sink into dirtiness!"

The king was amazed that his minister seemed to be able to read the mind of a horse. So he rewarded him appropriately.

The Buddha said:

"The royal horse in those days was this brother. Ānanda was the king. And I who have become the Buddha was the intelligent minister in those days."

The moral: "Even animals value cleanliness."

26

Ladyface
[Association]
(*Mahilāmukha-Jātaka*)

The Buddha told this story while he was living in Bamboo Grove temple with regard to Devadatta. One of the disciples of Sāriputta, instead of going to beg alms every day, was in the habit of going to Devadatta's temple for his meals. This news spread throughout the Bamboo Grove temple, and the story was learned by every monk. That monk was then brought before the Buddha. He admitted that daily he would take food at Devadatta's temple instead of following the vows that he had taken under the Buddha. The Buddha said, "Such was your nature even before." And the monks present asked the Buddha to tell the past story.

This is how it was:

Once upon time, the King of Benares had a royal bull elephant who was kind, patient and harmless. Along with his sweet disposition, he had a lovely gentle face. So he was affectionately known as 'Ladyface' [Mahilāmukha].

One night, a gang of robbers met together just outside the elephant shed. In the darkness they talked about their plans for robbing people. They spoke of beating and killing, and bragged that they had given up ordinary goodness so they would have no pity on their victims. They used rough he-man type gutter language, intended to scare people and show how tough they were.

Since the nights were quiet, Ladyface had nothing else to do but listen to all these terrible plans and violent rough talk. He listened carefully and, as elephants do, remembered it all. Having been brought up to obey and respect human beings, he thought these men were also to be obeyed and respected, even as teachers.

After this went on for several nights, Ladyface decided that the correct thing to do was to become rough and cruel. This usually happens to one who associates with those of a low-minded cruel nature. It happens especially to a gentle one who wishes to please others.

A 'mahout' is what the Indians call the special trainer and caretaker of a particular elephant. They are usually very close. Early one morning, Ladyface's mahout came to see him as usual. The elephant, his mind filled with the night's robber-talk, suddenly attacked his mahout. He picked him up in his trunk, squeezed the breath out of him, and smashed him to the ground, killing him instantly. Then he picked up two other attendants, one after another, and killed them just as ferociously.

Word spread quickly through the city that the once adored Ladyface had suddenly gone mad and become a frightening man killer. The people ran to the king for help.

It just so happened that the king had an intelligent minister who was known for his understanding of animals. So he called for him and asked him to go and determine what sickness or other condition had caused his favorite elephant to become so insanely violent.

This minister was the Bodhisatta – the Enlightenment Being. Arriving at the elephant shed, he spoke gentle soothing words to Ladyface, and calmed him down. He examined him and found him in perfect physical health. As he spoke kindly to Ladyface, he noticed that the elephant perked up his ears and paid very close attention. It was almost as if the poor animal were starved for the sound of gentle words. So the understanding minister figured out that the elephant must have been hearing the violent words or seeing the violent actions of those he mistook for teachers.

He asked the elephant guards, "Have you seen anyone hanging around this elephant shed, at night or any other time?" "Yes, minister," they replied, "for the last couple weeks a gang of robbers has been meeting here. We were afraid to do anything, since they were such mean rough characters. Ladyface could hear their every word."

The minister returned immediately to the king. He said, "My lord king, your favorite elephant, Ladyface, is in perfect physical health. I have discovered that it was by hearing the rough and vulgar talk of thieves during many nights, that he has learned to be violent and cruel. Unwholesome associations often lead to unwholesome thoughts and actions."

The king asked, "What is to be done?" The minister said, "Well my lord, now we must reverse the process. We must send wise men and monks, who have a high-minded kind nature, to spend just as many nights outside the elephant shed. There they should talk of the value of ordinary goodness and patience, leading to compassion, loving-kindness and harmlessness."

So it was carried out. For several nights the kind wise ones spoke of those wonderful qualities. They used only gentle and refined language, intended to bring peacefulness and comfort to others.

Lo and behold, hearing this pleasant conversation for several nights, Ladyface the bull elephant became even more peaceful and pleasant than before!

Seeing this total change, the minister reported it to the king, saying, "My lord, Ladyface is now even more harmless and sweet than before. Now he is as gentle as a lamb!"

The king said, "It is wonderful indeed that such a madly violent elephant can be changed by associating with wise men and monks." He was amazed that his minister seemed to be able to read the mind of an elephant. So he rewarded him appropriately.

The Buddha then connected the births in this way:

"The elephant that was influenced by whatever words he heard was this monk. The king was the Venerable Ānanda. And I who have become the Buddha was at that time the intelligent minister."

The moral: "As rough talk infects with violence, so do gentle words heal with harmlessness."

$\boxed{27}$

Best Friends
[The Power of Friendship]
(Abhiṇha-Jātaka)

The Buddha told this story while he was living in Jetavana temple about a lay disciple and an aged monk.

There were in the city of Sāvatthi two friends, one of whom became a monk but who used to go to the other's house each day for an alms of food. The Buddha mentioned that this friendship existed not only then, but also in the past. And the monks present asked the Buddha to tell the story.

The Buddha told the story in this way:

Before the time of this story, people in Asia used to say that there would never be a time when an elephant and a dog would be friends. Elephants simply did not like dogs, and dogs were afraid of elephants.

When dogs are frightened by those who are bigger than they are, they often bark very loudly, to cover up their fear. When dogs used to do this when they saw elephants, the elephants would get annoyed and chase them. Elephants had no patience at all when it came to dogs. Even if a dog were quiet and still, any nearby elephant would automatically attack him. This is why everybody agreed that elephants and dogs were 'natural enemies', just like lions and tigers, or cats and mice.

Once upon a time, there was a royal bull elephant, who was very well fed and cared for. In the neighborhood of the elephant shed, there was a scrawny, poorly fed, stray dog. He was attracted by the smell of the rich sweet rice being fed to the royal elephant. So he began sneaking into the shed and eating the wonderful rice that fell from the elephant's mouth. He liked it so much, that soon he would eat nowhere else. While enjoying his food, the big mighty elephant did not notice the tiny shy stray dog.

By eating such rich food, the once underfed dog gradually got bigger and stronger, and became very handsome looking. The good-natured elephant began to notice him. Since the dog had gotten used to being around the elephant, he had lost his fear. So he did not bark at him. Because he was not annoyed by the friendly dog, the elephant gradually got used to him.

Slowly they became friendlier and friendlier with each other. Before long, neither would eat without the other, and they enjoyed spending their time together. When they played, the dog would grab the elephant's heavy trunk, and the elephant would swing him forward and backward, from side to side, up and down, and even in circles! So it was that they became 'best friends', and wanted never to be separated.

Then one day a man from a remote village, who was visiting the city, passed by the elephant shed. He saw the frisky dog, who had become strong and beautiful. He bought him from the mahout, even though he didn't really own him. He took him back to his home village, without anyone knowing where that was.

Of course, the royal bull elephant became very sad, since he missed his best friend, the dog. He became so sad that he didn't want to do anything, not even eat or drink or bathe. So the mahout had to report this to the king, although he said nothing about selling the friendly dog.

It just so happened that the king had an intelligent minister who was known for his understanding of animals. So he told him to go and find out the reason for the elephant's condition.

The wise minister went to the elephant shed. He saw at once that the royal bull elephant was very sad. He thought, "This once happy elephant does not appear to be sick in any way. But I have seen this condition before, in men and animals alike. This elephant is grief-stricken, probably due to the loss of a very dear friend."

Then he said to the guards and attendants, "I find no sickness. He seems to be grief-stricken due to the loss of a friend. Do you know if this elephant had a very close friendship with anyone?"

They told him how the royal elephant and the stray dog were best friends. "What happened to this stray dog?" asked the minister. "He was taken by an unknown man," they replied, "and we do not know where he is now."

The minister returned to the king and said, "Your majesty, I am happy to say your elephant is not sick. As strange as it may sound, he became best friends with a stray dog! Since the dog has been taken away, the elephant is grief-stricken and does not feel like eating or drinking or bathing. This is my opinion."

The king said, "Friendship is one of life's most wonderful things. My minister, how can we bring back my elephant's friend and make him happy again?"

"My lord," replied the minister, "I suggest you make an official announcement, that whoever has the dog who used to live at the royal elephant shed, will be fined."

This was done, and when the villager heard of it, he released the dog from his house. He was filled with great happiness and ran as fast as he could, straight back to his best friend, the royal bull elephant.

The elephant was so overjoyed, that he picked up his friend with his trunk and sat him on top of his head. The happy dog wagged his tail, while the elephant's eyes sparkled with delight. They both lived happily ever after.

Meanwhile, the king was very pleased by his elephant's full recovery. He was amazed that his minister seemed to be able to read the mind of an elephant. So he rewarded him appropriately.

The Buddha connected the births, saying:

"The dog was the lay disciple. The elephant was this aged monk. And the wise minister was I who have today become the fully enlightened one."

The moral: "Even 'natural enemies' can become 'best friends'."

The Bull Called Delightful
[All Deserve Respect]
(Nandivisāla-Jātaka)

The Buddha told this story while dwelling at Jetavana temple about a group of six monks who spoke bitter words. These six monks used to taunt and jeer the other monks. This was complained about by the monks, and the Buddha summoned the six. He rebuked them, and said that even animals do not like being spoken to with harsh words. In order to explain himself more clearly, he told this story.

Once upon a time, in the country of Gandhāra in northern India, there was a city called Takkasilā.[21] In that city the Enlightenment Being was born as a certain calf. Since he was well bred for strength, he was bought by a high-class rich man. He became very fond of the gentle animal, and called him 'Delightful' [Nandivisāla]. He took good care of him and fed him only the best.

When Delightful grew up into a big fine strong bull, he thought, "I was brought up by this generous man. He gave me such good food and constant care, even though sometimes there were difficulties. Now I am a big grown up bull and there is no other bull who can pull as heavy a load as I can. Therefore, I would like to use my strength to give something in return to my master."

So he said to the man, "Sir, please find some wealthy merchant who is proud of having many strong bulls. Challenge him by saying that your bull can pull one hundred heavily loaded bullock carts."

---

21 Takkasilā, the capital of the kingdom of Gandhāra in the northwest of India, was a center of learning and trade in the Buddha's time. This was the city known as Taxila to Western classical writers.

Following his advice, the high-class rich man went to such a merchant and struck up a conversation. After a while, he brought up the idea of who had the strongest bull in the city.

The merchant said, "Many have bulls, but no one has any as strong as mine." The rich man said, "Sir, I have a bull who can pull one hundred heavily loaded bullock carts." "No, friend, how can there be such a bull? That is unbelievable!" said the merchant. The other replied, "I do have such a bull, and I am willing to make a bet."

The merchant said, "I will bet a thousand gold coins that your bull cannot pull a hundred loaded bullock carts." So the bet was made and they agreed on a date and time for the challenge.

The merchant attached together one hundred big bullock carts. He filled them with sand and gravel to make them very heavy.

The high-class rich man fed the finest rice to the bull called Delightful. He bathed him and decorated him and hung a beautiful garland of flowers around his neck.

Then he harnessed him to the first cart and climbed up onto it. Being so high-class, he could not resist the urge to make himself seem very important. So he cracked a whip in the air, and yelled at the faithful bull, "Pull, you dumb animal! I command you to pull, you big dummy!"

The bull called Delightful thought, "This challenge was my idea! I have never done anything bad to my master, and yet he insults me with such hard and harsh words!" So he remained in his place and refused to pull the carts.

The merchant laughed and demanded his winnings from the bet. The high-class rich man had to pay him the one thousand gold coins. He returned home and sat down, saddened by his lost bet, and embarrassed by the blow to his pride.

The bull called Delightful grazed peacefully on his way home. When he arrived, he saw his master sadly lying on his side. He asked, "Sir, why are you lying there like that? Are you sleeping? You look sad." The man said, "I lost a thousand gold coins because of you. With such a loss, how could I sleep?"

The bull replied, "Sir, you called me 'dummy'. You even cracked a whip in the air over my head. In all my life, did I ever break anything, step on anything, make a mess in the wrong place, or behave like a 'dummy' in any way?" He answered, "No, my pet."

The bull called Delightful said, "Then sir, why did you call me 'dumb animal', and insult me even in the presence of others? The fault is yours. I have done nothing wrong. But since I feel sorry for you, go again to the merchant and make the same bet for two thousand gold coins. And remember to use only the respectful words I deserve so well."

Then the high-class rich man went back to the merchant and made the bet for two thousand gold coins. The merchant thought it would be easy money. Again he set up the one hundred heavily loaded bullock carts. Again the rich man fed and bathed the bull, and hung a garland of flowers around his neck.

When all was ready, the rich man touched Delightful's forehead with a lotus blossom, having given up the whip. Thinking of him as fondly as if he were his own child, he said, "My son, please do me the honor of pulling these one hundred bullock carts."

Lo and behold, the wonderful bull pulled with all his might and dragged the heavy carts, until the last one stood in the place of the first.

The merchant, with his mouth hanging open in disbelief, had to pay the two thousand gold coins. The onlookers were so impressed that they honored the bull called Delightful with gifts. But even more important to the high-class rich man than his winnings, was his valuable lesson in humility and respect.

The Buddha said:

"The high-class rich man at that time is today Ānanda. And I myself was the bull called Delightful."

The moral: "Harsh words bring no reward. Respectful words bring honor to all."

$$\boxed{29}$$

Grandma's Blackie
[Loving-kindness]
(Kaṇha-Jātaka)

The Buddha told this story while dwelling at Jetavana temple after he had performed the three miracles.

The first miracle was removing doubt from the minds of the deities immediately after he had gained enlightenment. The second was overcoming the conceit of the elder Sakyā kinsmen after preaching about good and bad behavior. The third was creating the appearance of two opposites – fire and water, with the same cognition. After this, he went to heaven and preached what was to become the third part of the Theravāda Buddhist canon [the *Abhidhamma-Piṭaka*]. He then returned from heaven at Saṅkassa during the festival at the end of the rainy season, after which he went with a large following to Jetavana temple.

Gathering in the preaching hall, the monks praised the Buddha's miracles. When the Buddha entered, he asked, "Oh monks, what were you talking about before I came here?" The monks responded that they were talking about the Buddha's peerlessness. The Buddha then said, "Oh monks, not only today, but also in the past in my previous births as an animal I, too, was matchless."

And the Buddha then told this story of the past:

Once upon a time, when King Brahmadatta was ruling in Benares, there was an old woman who had a calf. This calf was of a noble dark color. In fact, he was jet black without a spot of white. He was the Bodhisatta – the Enlightenment Being.

The old woman raised the little calf just as though he were her own child. She fed him only the very best rice and rice porridge. She petted his head and neck, and he licked her hand. Since they were so friendly, the people began calling the calf, 'Grandma's Blackie [Kaṇha]'.

Even after he grew up into a big strong bull, Grandma's Blackie remained very tame and gentle. The village children played with him, holding onto his neck and ears and horns. They would even grab his tail and swing up onto his back for a ride. He liked children, so he never complained.

The friendly bull thought, "The loving old woman, who brought me up, is like a kind mother to me. She raised me as if I were her own child. She is poor and in need, but too humble to ask for my help. She is too gentle to force me to work. Because I also love her, I wish to release her from the suffering of poverty." So he began looking for work.

One day a caravan of 500 carts came by the village. It stopped at a difficult place to cross the river. The bullocks were not able to pull the carts across. The caravan leader hooked up all 500 pairs of bullocks to the first cart. But the river was so rough that they could not pull across even that one cart.

Faced with this problem, the leader began looking for more bulls. He was known to be an expert judge of the qualities of bulls. While examining the wandering village herd, he noticed Grandma's Blackie. At once he thought, "This noble bullock looks like he has the strength and the will to pull my carts across the river."

He said to the villagers standing nearby, "To whom does this big black bull belong? I would like to use him to pull my caravan across the river, and I am willing to pay his owner for his services." The people said, "By all means, take him. His master is not here."

So he put a rope through Grandma's Blackie's nose. But when he pulled, he could not budge him! The bull was thinking, "Until this man says what he will pay for my work, I will not move."

Being such a good judge of bulls, the caravan leader understood his reasoning. So he said, "My dear bull, after you have pulled my 500 carts across the river, I will pay you two gold coins for each cart – not just one, but two!" Hearing this, Grandma's Blackie went with him at once.

Then the man harnessed the strong black bull to the first cart. He proceeded to pull it across the river. This was what all one thousand bulls could not do before. Likewise, he pulled across each of the other 499 carts, one at a time, without slowing down a bit!

When all was done, the caravan leader made a package containing only one gold coin per cart, that is, 500 coins. He hung this around the mighty bullock's neck. The bull thought, "This man promised two gold coins per cart, but that is not what he has hung around my neck. So I will not let him leave!" He went to the front of the caravan and blocked the path.

The leader tried to push him out of the way, but he would not move. He tried to drive the carts around him. But all the bulls had seen how strong he was, so they would not move either!

The man thought, "There is no doubt that this is a very intelligent bull, who knows I have given him only half-pay." So he made a new package containing the full one thousand gold coins, and hung it instead around the bull's neck.

Then Grandma's Blackie re-crossed the river and walked directly towards the old woman, his 'mother'. Along the way, the children tried to grab the money package, thinking it was a game. But he escaped them.

When the woman saw the heavy package, she was surprised. The children told her all about what happened down at the river. She opened the package and discovered the one thousand gold coins.

The old woman also saw the tired look in the eyes of her 'child'. She said, "Oh my son, do you think I wish to live off the money you earn? Why did you wish to work so hard and suffer so? No matter how difficult it may be, I will always care for and look after you."

Then the kind woman washed the lovely bull and massaged his tired muscles with oil. She fed him good food and cared for him, until the end of their happy lives together.

The Buddha said:

"The old woman was Uppalavaṇṇā. And Grandma's Blackie was I who have become the Buddha."

The moral: "Loving-kindness makes the poorest house into the richest home."

30, 286

Big Red, Little Red and No-squeal
[Envy]
(Muṇika-Jātaka)

The Buddha told this story while living at Jetavana monastery about a monk who wished to disrobe on account of an unmarried girl. The Buddha summoned that monk and asked, "Is it true that you are infatuated with a young girl, and that you desire to be disrobed because of this?" The Buddha said, "You have gotten into trouble in the past also because of this girl. This girl is trouble for you. In the past because of her, your flesh became curry to eat." And saying this, the Buddha told the story.

Once upon a time, there were two calves who were part of a country household. At the same home there also lived a girl and a baby pig. Since he hardly ever made a sound, the pig was called 'No-squeal' [Muṇika].

The masters of the house treated No-squeal very, very well. They fed him large amounts of the very best rice, and even rice porridge with rich brown sugar.

The two calves noticed this. They worked hard pulling plows in the fields and bullock carts on the roads. Little Red [Cullalohita] said to Big Red [Mahālohita], "My big brother, in this household you and I do all the hard work. We bring prosperity to the family. But they feed us only grass and hay. The baby pig No-squeal does nothing to support the family. And yet they feed him the finest and fanciest of foods. Why should he get such special treatment?"

The wise elder brother said, "Oh young one, it is dangerous to envy anybody. Therefore, do not envy the baby pig for being fed such rich food. What he eats is really 'the food of death'.

"There will soon be a marriage ceremony for the daughter of the house, and little No-squeal will be the wedding feast! That's why he is being pampered and fed in such rich fashion.

"In a few days the guests will arrive. Then this piglet will be dragged away by the legs, killed, and made into curry for the feast."

Sure enough, in a few days the wedding guests arrived. The baby pig No-squeal was dragged away and killed. And just as Big Red had said, he was cooked in various types of curries and devoured by the guests.

Then Big Red said, "My dear young brother, did you see what happened to baby No-squeal?" "Yes brother," replied Little Red, "now I understand."

Big Red continued, "This is the result of being fed such rich food. Our poor grass and hay are a hundred times better than his rich porridge and sweet brown sugar. For our food brings no harm to us, but instead promises long life!"

The Buddha then identified the births in this way:

"The pig named No-squeal was this monk. Little Red was the Venerable Ānanda. And Big Red was I who have become the Buddha."

The moral: "Don't envy the well-off, until you know the price they pay."

The Heaven of 33
(Kulāvaka-Jātaka)

The Buddha told this story while dwelling at Jetavana monastery about a monk who drank water without straining it.

Tradition has it that two young brothers who were on good terms with one another went from Sāvatthi into the countryside, where they stayed for a long time. They then set out for Jetavanārāma to see the Buddha.

One of them carried a strainer to strain his water, and the other one didn't. And so they shared the same strainer before drinking. Then, on the way, they argued. And the brother who owned the strainer would not let the other use it. The other brother, because he became very thirsty, drank water without straining it.

When they reached Jetavanārāma, they went to see the Buddha. After giving him a respectful salutation, they took seats to his side. "Bhante," they said, "we have come to see you from where we have been living in the countryside in Kosala state." The Buddha asked, "Did you remain good friends along the way?" The brother without a strainer said, "Bhante, on the way we had an argument, and my brother would not give me his strainer." Then the Buddha asked, "Then, knowingly, you drank water with living creatures? Did you do so?" "Yes Bhante, I did drink unstrained water." The Buddha said, "Oh monk, in the past wise and good people, when flying to escape the ugly gods called Asura-s who had gained sovereignty over the city of the gods refrained from killing living creatures. Instead, they turned their chariot back in order to save the lives of young Garuḷa-birds, and because of this gained power for themselves."

And the Buddha told this story of the past:

Chapter 1. Cooperation

Once upon a time, when King Magadha was ruling in the land, there was a young noble called, 'Magha the Good'. He lived in a remote village of just 30 families. When he was young, his parents married him to a girl who had qualities of character similar to his own. They were very happy together, and she gave birth to several children.

The villagers came to respect Magha the Good because he always tried to help improve the village, for the good of all. Because they respected him, he was able to teach the five steps of training [*pañca-sīla-s*, the first five *sikkhā-pada-s*], to purify their thoughts, words and deeds.

Magha's way of teaching was by doing. An example of this happened one day when the villagers gathered to do handicraft work. Magha the Good cleaned a place for himself to sit. Before he could sit down though, someone else sat there. So he patiently cleaned another place. Again a neighbor sat in his place. This happened over and over again, until he had patiently cleaned sitting places for all those present. Only then could he himself sit in the last place.

By using such examples of patience, Magha the Good taught his fellow villagers how to cooperate with each other, without quarreling. Working together in this way, they constructed several buildings and made other improvements that benefited the whole village.

Seeing the worthwhile results of patience and cooperation, based on following the gentle ways of the Five Training Steps, all in the village became calmer and more peaceful. A natural side effect was that former crimes and wrongdoing completely disappeared!

You would think this would make everybody happier. However, there was one man who did not like the new situation at all. He was the head of the village, the politician who cared only about his own position.

Formerly, when there were murders and thefts, he handed out punishments. This increased his position of authority, and caused the villagers to fear him. When husbands or wives had affairs with others, the headman collected fines. In the same way, when reputations were damaged by lies, or contracts were not lived up to, he also collected fines. He even got tax money from the profits of selling strong liquor. He did not mind that drunkenness led to many of the crimes.

It is easy to see why the headman was upset to lose so much respect and power and money, due to the people living peacefully together. So he went to the king and said, "My lord, some of the remote villages are being robbed and looted by bandits. We need your help."

The king said, "Bring all these criminals to me."

The dishonest politician rounded up the heads of all 30 families and brought them as prisoners to the king. Without questioning them, the king ordered that they all be trampled to death by elephants.

All 30 were ordered to lie down in the palace courtyard and the elephants were brought in. They realized they were about to be trampled to death. Magha the Good said to them, "Remember and concentrate on the peacefulness and purity that come from following the Five Training Steps, so you may feel loving-kindness [*mettā*] towards all. In this way, do not get angry at the unjust king, the lying headman, or the unfortunate elephants."

The first elephant was brought in by his mahout. But when he tried to force him to trample the innocent villagers, the elephant refused. He trumpeted as he went away. Amazingly, this was repeated with each of the king's elephants. None would step on them.

The mahouts complained to the king that this was not their fault. "It must be," they said, "that these men have some drug that is confusing the elephants."

The king had the villagers searched, but they found nothing. Then his advisers said, "These men must be magicians who have cast an evil spell on your mighty elephants!"

The villagers were asked, "Do you have such a spell?" Magha the Good said, "Yes, we do." This made the king very curious. So he himself asked Magha, "What is this spell and how does it work?"

Magha the Good replied, "My lord king, we do not cast the same kinds of spells that others cast. We cast the spell of loving-kindness with minds made pure by following the Five Training Steps."

"What are these Five Training Steps?" asked the king. Magha the Good said, "All of us have given up the five unwholesome actions, which are: destroying life, taking what is not given, doing wrong in sexual ways, speaking falsely, and losing one's mind from alcohol.

"In this way we have become harmless, so that we can give the gift of fearlessness to all. Therefore, the elephants lost their fear of the mahouts, and did not wish to harm us. They departed, trumpeting triumphantly. This was our protection, which you have called a 'spell'."

Finally seeing the wholesomeness and wisdom of these people, the king questioned them and learned the truth. He decided to confiscate all the property of the dishonest village headman and divide it among them.

The villagers were then free to do even more good works for the benefit of the whole village. Soon they began to build a big roadside inn, right next to the highway crossroads.

This was the biggest project they had yet undertaken. The men were confident because they had learned so well how to cooperate with each other for a common goal. But they had not yet learned how to cooperate in this work with the women of the village. They seemed to think it was 'man's work'.

By this time Magha the Good had four wives. Their names were Good-doer [Sudhammā], Beauty [Cittā], Happy [Nandā] and Well-born [Sujātā]. Of these, the first wife, Good-doer, was the wisest. She wanted to pave the way for the women to benefit from cooperating in doing good work. So she gradually became friendly with the boss in charge of the roadside inn project.

Because she wanted to contribute by helping in a big way, she gave a present to the boss. She asked him, "Can you think of a way that I may become the most important contributor to this good work?"

The boss replied, "I know just such a way!" Then he secretly constructed the most important part of the building, the roof beam that would hold the roof together. He wrapped it up and hid it with Good-doer, so it could dry for the time necessary to become rigid and strong.

Meanwhile, the men of the village continued happily in the building project. At last they got to the point of installing the roof beam. They began to make one, but the boss interrupted them. He said, "My friends, we cannot use fresh green wood to make the roof beam. It will bend and sag. We must have an aged dry roof beam. Go find one!"

When they searched in the village, they found that Good-doer just happened to have a perfect roof beam. It was even the right size! When they asked if they could buy it from her, she said, "It is not for sale at any price. I wish to contribute the roof beam for free, but only if you let me participate in building the inn."

The men were afraid to change their successful ways. So they said, "Women have never been part of this project. This is impossible."

Then they returned to the construction boss and told him what had happened. He said, "Why do you keep the women away? Women are part of everything in this world. Let us be generous and share the harmony and wholesomeness of this work with the women. Then the project and our village will be even more successful."

So they accepted the roof beam from Good-doer, and she helped to finish the building of the inn. Then Beauty had a wonderful garden built next to the inn, which she donated. It had all kinds of flowers and fruit trees. So too, Happy had a lovely pond dug, and planted beautiful lotuses in it. But Well-born, being the youngest and a little spoiled, did nothing for the inn.

In the evenings, Magha the Good held meetings in the roadside inn. He taught the people to assist their parents and elders, and to give up harsh words, accusing others behind their backs, and being stingy.

It is said that the lowest heaven world contains the gods of the four directions, North, East, South and West. Because he followed his

own teachings, Magha the Good died with happiness in his heart. He was reborn as Sakka, king of the second lowest heaven world.

In time, the heads of all the other families of the village, as well as Good-doer, Beauty and Happy, also died. They were reborn as gods under King Sakka. This was known as the 'Heaven of 33'.

Chapter 2. Compassion

At that time, so very long ago, there were some unfortunate ugly gods called 'Asura-s'. They had taken to living in the second heaven world.

The one who had been Magha the Good in his previous life, was now Sakka, King of the Heaven of 33. He thought, "Why should we, who are the 33, live in our Heaven of 33 with these unfortunate ugly Asura-s? Since this is our world, let us live happily by ourselves."

So he invited them to a party and got them drunk on very strong liquor. It seems that, in being reborn, King Sakka had forgotten some of his own teachings as Magha the Good. After getting the Asura-s drunk, he got them to go to a lower world, just as big as the Heaven of 33.

When they sobered up and realized they had been tricked into going to a lower heaven world, the Asura-s became angry. They rose up and made war against King Sakka. Soon they were victorious, and Sakka was forced to run away.

While retreating in his mighty war chariot, he came to the vast forest where the Garuḷa-s have their nests. These are gods who, unfortunately, have no super powers. Instead they are forced to get around by flapping huge heavy wings.

When King Sakka's chariot drove through their forest, it upset their nests and made the baby Garuḷa-s fall down. They cried in fear and agony. Hearing this, Sakka asked his charioteer Mātali where these sad cries were coming from. Mātali answered, "These are the shrieks of terror coming from the baby Garuḷa-s, whose nests and trees are being destroyed by your powerful war chariot."

Hearing this suffering, King Sakka realized that all lives, including his own, are only temporary. Hearing this suffering, the compassion of the Great Being [Bodhisatta], which passes from life to life, arose within him and said, "Let the little ones have no more fear. The first training step must not be broken. There can be no exception. I will not destroy even one

life for the sake of a heavenly kingdom that must some day end. Instead I will offer my life to the victorious Asura-s. Turn back the chariot!"

So the chariot returned in the direction of the Heaven of 33. The Asura-s saw King Sakka turn around, and thought he must have reinforcements from other worlds. So they ran, without looking back, down to their lower heaven world.

Chapter 3. Merit

King Sakka returned victoriously to his palace in the Heaven of 33. Next to it stood the mansion of his first wife, the reborn Good-doer. Outside the mansion was the garden of his second wife, the reborn Beauty. And there was the heavenly pond of his third wife, the reborn Happy.

However, Well-born had died and been reborn as a slender crane in the forest. Since he missed her, Sakka found her and brought her up to the Heaven of 33 for a visit. He showed her the mansion and the garden and the pond of his three wives. He told her that, by doing good work, the other three had gained merit. This merit had brought them happiness, both in their previous lives and in their rebirths.

He said, "You, my dear crane, in your previous life as Well-born, did no such good work. So you did not gain either merit or happiness, and were reborn as a forest crane. I advise you to begin on the path of purity by following the Five Training Steps." After being taught the five steps, the lovely crane decided to follow them. Then she returned to the forest.

Not long afterwards, King Sakka was curious about how the crane was doing. So he took the shape of a fish and lay down in front of her. The crane picked him up by the head. She was just about to swallow the King of the Heaven of 33, when the fish wiggled his tail.

Immediately the crane thought, "This fish must be alive!" Remembering the first training step, she released the living fish back into the stream. Rising from the water, King Sakka returned to his godly form and said, "It is very good, my dear crane, that you are able to follow the Five Training Steps." Then he returned to the second heaven world.

In the fullness of time, the crane died. Following the Five Training Steps had brought her both merit and a peaceful mind. So she was reborn in the wonderful state of mankind, into a potter's family in Benares, in northern India.

Again King Sakka was interested in finding out where the one who had been Well-born, and then the crane, was now reborn. He found her in the potter's family, and wanted to help her in gaining merit and finding happiness.

So he disguised himself as an old man and created a cart full of golden cucumbers. He went into Benares and shouted, "Cucumbers! Cucumbers! I have cucumbers!"

When people came to buy these amazing cucumbers, he said, "These golden cucumbers are not for sale. I will give them away, but only to one who is wholesome, that is, one who follows the Five Training Steps."

The people said, "We never heard of the Five Training Steps. But we will buy your golden cucumbers. Name your price!" He repeated, "My cucumbers are not for sale. I have brought them to give to any person who practices the Five Training Steps." The people said, "This man has come here only to play tricks on us." So they left him alone.

Soon Well-born heard about this unusual man. Even though she had been reborn, she still had the habit of following the Five Training Steps. So she thought, "This man must have come to find me."

She went to him and asked for the golden cucumbers. He said, "Do you follow the Five Training Steps? Have you given up destroying life, taking what is not given, doing wrong in sexual ways, speaking falsely, and losing your mind from alcohol?" She answered, "Yes sir, I do follow these steps, and I am peaceful and happy."

Then the old man said, "I brought these cucumbers especially for you, to encourage you to gain more merit and future happiness." So he left the cart of golden cucumbers with her, and returned to the Heaven of 33.

Throughout the rest of her life, the woman was very generous with all this gold. Spreading her happiness to others, she gained merit. After she died, she was reborn as the daughter of the King of the Asura-s. She grew up to be a goddess of great beauty. To the Asura-s this seemed like a miracle, since the rest of them were the ugliest of all the gods.

The Asura king was pleased with his daughter's goodness, as well as her famous beauty. He gathered all the Asura-s together and gave her the freedom to choose a husband.

Sakka, King of the Heaven of 33, knew of the latest rebirth of the one who had been his wife Well-born, then a crane, and then a potter's daughter. So he came down to the lower heaven world and took the shape of an ordinary ugly Asura. He thought, "If Well-born chooses a husband whose inner qualities of wholesomeness are the same as hers, we will be reunited at last!"

Because of her past associations with Magha the Good, reborn as King Sakka, now disguised as an ordinary Asura, the beautiful princess was drawn to him. So she picked him from among all the Asura-s.

King Sakka took her to the Heaven of 33, made her his fourth wife, and they lived happily ever after.

* * *

The Buddha then said:

"The charioteer Mātali at that time was the Venerable Ānanda. And King Sakka, who in his previous life was Magha the Good, was I who have become the Buddha."

The moral: "The Five Training Steps are the beginning of wholesomeness. Wholesomeness is the beginning of peace and happiness."

32

The Dancing Peacock
[Pride and Modesty]
(Nacca-Jātaka)

When the Buddha was dwelling at Jetavana monastery, he told this story on account of a certain shameless monk. This monk collected robes, linens, and such belongings. Some visiting monks saw this and told him that by doing so, he was both displaying and developing craving for material things. Hearing this, he discarded these things and stark naked left the temple to become again a layman.

One day, the monks were talking about this incident in the preaching hall. When the Buddha came there, he asked, "Oh monks, about what were you talking before I came here?" The monks replied, "Bhante, we were talking about the monk who collected robes, and discarding them, left naked to become again a layman." The Buddha said, "Oh monks, not only now has be behaved shamelessly like this. In the past also he lost his gains, and also lost a good woman." And without invitation, the Buddha told this story:

Once upon a time, a very long time ago, the four-footed animals made the lion their king. There was a gigantic fish that roamed the oceans, and the fish made him their king. The birds were attracted to beauty, so they chose the Golden Swan as their king.

King Golden Swan had a beautiful golden daughter. While she was still young, he granted her one wish. She wished that, when she was old enough, she could pick her own husband.

When his daughter was old enough, King Golden Swan called all the birds living in the vast Himalayan Mountains of central Asia to a gathering. The purpose was to find a worthy husband for his golden daughter. Birds came from far away, even from high Tibet. There were geese, swans, eagles, sparrows, humming birds, cuckoos, owls and many other kinds of birds.

The gathering was held on a high rock slab, in the beautiful green land of Nepal. King Golden Swan told his lovely daughter to select whichever husband she wished.

She looked over the many birds. Her eye was attracted by a shining emerald-green long-necked peacock, with gorgeous flowing tail feathers. She told her father, "This bird, the peacock, will be my husband."

Hearing that he was the lucky one, all the other birds crowded around the peacock to congratulate him. They said, "Even among so many beautiful birds, the golden swan princess has chosen you. We congratulate you on your good fortune."

The peacock became so puffed up with pride, that he began to show off his colorful feathers in a fantastic strutting dance. He fanned out his spectacular tail feathers and danced in a circle to show off his beautiful tail. Being so conceited, he pointed his head at the sky and forgot all modesty, so that he also showed his most private parts for all to see!

The other birds, especially the young ones, giggled. But King Golden Swan was not amused. He was embarrassed to see his daughter's choice behave in this way. He thought, "This peacock has no inner shame to give him proper modesty. Nor does he have the outer fear to prevent indecent behavior. So why should my daughter be shamed by such a mindless mate?"

Standing in the midst of the great assembly of birds, the king said, "Sir peacock, your voice is sweet, your feathers are beautiful, your neck shines like an emerald, and your tail is like a splendid fan. But you have danced here like one who has no proper shame or fear. I will not permit my innocent daughter to marry such an ignorant fool!"

Then King Golden Swan married his golden daughter to a royal nephew. The silly strutting peacock flew away, having lost a beautiful wife.

The Buddha then said:

"The shameless monk was at that time the peacock. And I who have become the Buddha was King Golden Swan at that time."

The moral: "If you let pride go to your head, you'll wind up acting like a fool."

33

The Quail King and the Hunter
[Unity]
(*Sammodamāna-Jātaka, Vaṭṭaka-Jātaka*)

The Buddha told this story when he was living in the banyan tree grove near the city of Kapilavatthu in Nepal. The circumstances of its narration are told further on in this collection of Jātaka tales in the *Kuṇāla-Jātaka* [No. 536].

[This story (the *Kuṇāla-Jātaka*) was told with regard to the river Rohiṇī, which flowed between the cities of Kapilavatthu and Koliya. The Sakyā and Koliya tribes, both kinsmen of the Buddha, used the water of this river to cultivate their crops. At one time, an argument grew up between these two tribes as to the use of this water. Each argued that the water was not sufficient to water the crops of both tribes, but that their crops would thrive with a single watering. So, the other should let them take the water. And they began to exchange blows and disrespectful words. This led to their taking up arms against one another.

At that time, the Buddha was dwelling in Sāvatthi. Seeing them setting out to fight one another with his divine eye, he thought that he might be able to quell the feud if he went there.

Going there, he sat cross-legged in the sky between the two groups of combatants, which at first startled them. When each party saw that this was their kinsman, the Buddha, they each laid down their arms. Then the Buddha descended to a magnificent throne. And the nobles of the two sides, paying reverence to him, took seats to his side. The Buddha then asked them what the quarrel was about. They told him that it was about the water. He asked them, "What is the water worth?" They responded, "Very little, Bhante." He then asked, "What is the earth worth?" The responded, "It is priceless." The Buddha asked, "What are warrior nobles worth?" They responded, "They, too, are priceless." The Buddha then said, "Why on account of some worthless water are you setting out to destroy nobles of high worth?" And the Buddha then related five Jātaka stories to illustrate the result of unity, one of which was the *Sammodamāna-Jātaka.* ...]

The Buddha spoke to his relatives, saying, "Oh relatives, it is not good for you to argue. Even in the past, animals who lived together harmoniously came to destruction when they argued. And then his relatives asked the Buddha to relate this past story.

The Buddha said:

Once upon a time, there was a Quail King who reigned over a flock of a thousand quails.

There was also a very clever quail hunter. He knew how to make a quail call. Because this sounded just like a real quail crying for help, it never failed to attract other quails. Then the hunter covered them with a net, stuffed them in baskets, and sold them to make a living.

Because he always put the safety of his flock first, Quail King was highly respected by all. While on the lookout for danger, one day he came across the hunter and saw what he did. He thought, "This quail hunter has a good plan for destroying our relatives. I must make a better plan to save us."

Then he called together his whole nation of a thousand quails. He also invited other quails to attend the meeting. He said, "Greetings to our quail nation and welcome to our visitors. We are faced with great danger. Many of our relatives are being trapped and sold by a clever hunter. Then they are being killed and eaten. I have come up with a plan to save us all. When the hunter covers us with his net, every single one of us must raise his neck at the same time. Then, all together, we should fly away with the net and drop it on a thorn bush. That will keep him busy, and we will be able to escape with our lives." All agreed to follow this smart strategy.

The next day the hunter lured the quails with his quail call as usual.

But when he threw his net over them, they all raised up their necks at once, flew away with the net, and dropped it on a thorn bush. He could catch no quails at all! In addition, it took him the rest of the day to loosen his net from the thorns – so he had no time left to try again!

The same thing happened on the following day. So he spent a second day unhooking his net from sharp thorns. He arrived home only to be greeted by his wife's sharp tongue! She complained, "You used to bring home quail to eat, and money from selling quails. Now you return empty-handed. What do you do all day? You must have another wife somewhere, who is feasting on quail meat at this very moment!"

The hunter replied, "Don't think such a thing, my darling. These days the quails have become very unified. They act as one, and raise up their necks and carry my net to a thorn bush. But thanks to you, my one and only wife, I know just what to do! Just as you argue with me, one day they too will argue, as relatives usually do. While they are occupied in conflict and bickering, I will trap them and bring them back to you. Then you will be pleased with me again. Until then, I must be patient."

The hunter had to put up with his wife's complaints for several more days. Then one morning, after being lured by the quail call, it just so happened that one quail accidentally stepped on the head of another. He immediately got angry and squawked at her. She removed her foot from his head and said, "Please don't be angry with me. Please excuse my mistake." But he would not listen. Soon both of them were squawking and squawking, and the conflict got worse and worse!

Hearing this bickering getting louder and louder, Quail King said, "There is no advantage in conflict. Continuing it will lead to danger!" But they just wouldn't listen.

Then Quail King thought, "I'm afraid this silly conflict will keep them from cooperating to raise the net." So he commanded that all should escape. His own flock flew away at once.

And it was just in time too! Suddenly the quail hunter threw his net over the remaining quails. The two arguing quails said to each other, "I

won't hold the net for you!" Hearing this, even some of the other quails said, "Why should I hold the net for anyone else?"

So the conflict spread like wildfire. The hunter grabbed all the quails, stuffed them in his baskets, and took them home to his wife. Of course she was overjoyed, and they invited all their friends over for a big quail feast.

The Buddha then ended this Jātaka story, saying:

"The wise Quail King at that time was I who am today the Buddha."

The moral: "There is safety in unity, and danger in conflict."

The Fortunate Fish
[Desire]
(Maccha-Jātaka)

The Buddha delivered this story when he was living in Jetavana monastery with regard to a certain monk who was lovesick for his former wife.

The Buddha saw that this monk was confused about his monkhood, and asked this monk, "Is it true that you still desire your former wife?" The monk answered, "Yes, Bhante." The Buddha then said, "Oh monk, on account of this woman in a previous birth as well, you fell into trouble. But I saved you." And the Buddha then told this story of the past:

Once upon a time, King Brahmadatta had a very wise adviser who understood the speech of animals. He understood what they said, and he could speak to them in their languages.

One day the adviser was wandering along the riverbank with his followers. They came upon some fishermen who had cast a big net into the river. While peering into the water, they noticed a big handsome fish who was following his pretty wife.

Her shining scales reflected the morning sunlight in all the colors of the rainbow. Her feather-like fins fluttered like the delicate wings of a fairy, as they sent her gliding through the water. It was clear that her husband was so entranced by the way she looked and the way she moved, that he was not paying attention to anything else!

As they came near the net, the wife fish smelled it. Then she saw it and alertly avoided it at the very last moment. But her husband was so blinded by his desire for her, that he could not turn away fast enough.

Instead, he swam right into the net and was trapped!

The fishermen pulled in their net and threw the big fish onto the shore. They built a fire, and carved a spit to roast him on.

Lying on the ground, the fish was flopping around and groaning in agony. Since the wise adviser understood fish talk, he translated for the others. He said, "This poor fish is madly repeating over and over again:

'My wife! My wife! I must be with my wife!
I care for her much more than for my life!
'My wife! My wife! I must be with my wife!
I care for her much more than for my life!'"

The adviser thought, "Truly this fish has gone crazy. He is in this terrible state because he became a slave to his own desire. And it is clear that he has learned nothing from the results of his actions. If he dies keeping such agony, and the desire that caused it, in his mind, he will surely continue to suffer by being reborn in some hell world. Therefore, I must save him!"

So this kind man went over to the fishermen and said, "Oh my friends, loyal subjects of our king, you have never given me and my followers a fish for our curry. Won't you give us one today?"

They replied, "Oh royal minister, please accept from us any fish you wish!" "This big one on the riverbank looks delicious," said the adviser. "Please take him, sir," they said.

Then he sat down on the bank. He took the fish, who was still groaning, into his hands. He spoke to him in the language only fish can understand, saying, "You foolish fish! If I had not seen you today, you would have gotten yourself killed. Your blind desire was leading you to continued suffering. From now on, do not let yourself be trapped by your own desires!"

Then the fish realized how fortunate he was to have found such a friend. He thanked him for his wise advice. The minister released the lucky fish back into the river, and went on his way.

The Buddha then connected the births:

"The female fish was the wife of this lovesick monk. The lovesick monk was the male fish. And the very wise adviser who saved the fish's life was I who have become the Buddha."

The moral: "Fools are trapped by their own desires."

35

The Baby Quail Who Could Not Fly Away [The Power of Truth, Wholesomeness and Compassion]
(Vaṭṭaka-Jātaka)

Once, when the Buddha was going to Magadha with a group of monks, there was a fire in the forest on the way. This story was told with regard to this fire.

At the time, the monks who were not yet saintly became afraid of the fire. But when the fire came near the Buddha, it miraculously disappeared, as if water had been put on it. Then all the monks, together, began to praise the Buddha. Hearing their appreciation, the Buddha said, "Oh monks, this is not due to my present merit. In a previous life, also, fire in this spot was extinguished by me due to the power of Truth [sacca-kiriyā]. Because of this, fire will always go out in this spot." Then, the monks requested the Buddha to disclose the previous story.

This is how it was:

Once upon a time, the Enlightenment Being was born as a tiny quail. Although he had little feet and wings, he could not yet walk or fly. His parents worked hard bringing food to the nest, feeding him from their beaks.

In that part of the world, there were usually forest fires every year. So it happened that a fire began in that particular year. All the birds who were able, flew away at the first sign of smoke. As the fire spread, and got closer and closer to the nest of the baby quail, his parents remained with him. Finally the fire got so close, that they too had to fly away to save their lives.

All the trees, big and small, were burning and crackling with a loud noise. The little one saw that everything was being destroyed by the fire that raged out of control. He could do nothing to save himself. At that moment, his mind was overwhelmed by a feeling of helplessness.

Then it occurred to him, "My parents loved me very much. Unselfishly they built a nest for me, and then fed me without greed. When the fire came, they remained with me until the last moment. All the other birds who could, had flown away a long time before.

"So great was the loving-kindness [*mettā*] of my parents, that they stayed and risked their lives, but still they were helpless to save me. Since they could not carry me, they were forced to fly away alone. I thank them, wherever they are, for loving me so. I hope with all my heart they will be safe and well and happy.

"Now I am all alone. There is no one I can go to for help. I have wings, but I cannot fly away. I have feet, but I cannot run away. But I can still think. All I have left to use is my mind – a mind that remains pure. The only beings I have known in my short life were my parents, and my mind has been filled with loving-kindness towards them. I have done nothing unwholesome to anyone. I am filled with newborn innocent truthfulness."

Then an amazing miracle took place. This innocent truthfulness grew and grew until it became larger than the little baby bird. The knowledge of truth spread beyond that one lifetime, and many previous births became known. One such previous birth had led to knowing a Buddha, a fully enlightened knower of Truth [Dhamma] – one who had the power of Truth [Saccaṁ], the purity of wholesomeness, and the purpose of compassion.

Then the Great Being [Bodhisatta] within the tiny baby quail thought, "May this very young innocent truthfulness be united with that ancient purity of wholesomeness and power of Truth. May all birds and other beings, who are still trapped by the fire, be saved. And may this spot be safe from fire for a million years!"

And so it was.

The Buddha said:

"The tiny baby quail was I who have today become the fully enlightened one."

The moral: "Truth, wholesomeness and compassion can save the world."

36

Wise Birds and Foolish Birds
[Good Advice]
(Sakuṇa-Jātaka)

When the Buddha was living in Jetavana monastery in Sāvatthi, he told this story on account of a monk's burned down hermitage. The people in the nearby village promised to repair the hermitage, but they kept postponing it. Even after three months time, the villagers did not repair it. And because of this, the monk could not advance his mental state through his meditation for the course of the entire rainy season.

After the three months of the rainy season, the monk went back to Sāvatthi to see the Buddha. The Buddha heard from him what had happened, and he said, "You ought to be ashamed of yourself. Even birds in the past knew to leave a place where there was fire. Why did you not know that you should leave such a place?"

All the monks present asked the Buddha to relate the story of the past.

The Buddha told the story in this way:

Once upon a time, there was a giant tree in the forest. Many, many birds lived in this tree. And the wisest of them was their leader.

One day the leader bird saw two branches rubbing against each other. They were making wood powder come falling down. Then he noticed a tiny wisp of smoke rising from the rubbing branches. He thought, "There is no doubt a fire is starting that may burn down the whole forest."

So the wise old leader called a meeting of all the birds living in the great tree. He told them, "My dear friends, the tree we are living in is beginning to make a fire. This fire may destroy the whole forest. Therefore, it is dangerous to stay here. Let us leave this forest at once!"

The wise birds agreed to follow his advice. So they flew away to another forest in a different land. But the birds who were not so wise said, "That old leader panics so easily. He imagines crocodiles in a drop of water! Why should we leave our comfortable homes that have always been safe? Let the scared ones go. We will be brave and trust in our tree!"

Lo and behold, in a little while the wise leader's warning came true. The rubbing branches made sparks that fell in the dry leaves under the tree. Those sparks became flames that grew and grew. Soon the giant tree itself caught fire. The foolish birds who still lived there were blinded and choked by the smoke. Many, who could not escape, were trapped and burned to death.

The Buddha then ended this Jātaka story, saying:

"The birds who flew away, listening to their wise leader's advice, are today my disciples. And their wise old leader was I who have today become the fully enlightened Buddha."

The moral: "Those who ignore the advice of the wise do so at their own risk."

37

The Birth of a Banyan Tree
[Respect for Elders]
(*Tittira-Jātaka*)

When the Buddha was on his way to Jetavana monastery in Sāvatthi, a certain group of six elders went ahead and together with their followers, occupied all the rooms. Even the Venerable Sāriputta, the Buddha's chief disciple, had no room available for him, and so he spent the night under a tree. Seeing this, the Buddha questioned about the situation and learned what had happened. He then admonished the followers of the group of six elders and told them that they ought to defer to their elders, and respect them. Such was done even by animals in the past. And the monks asked the Buddha to tell the story of the past.

The Buddha told the past story in this way:

Once upon a time, there was a big banyan tree in the forest beneath the mighty Himalayas. Living near this banyan tree were three very good friends. They were a quail, a monkey and an elephant. Each of them was quite smart.

Occasionally the three friends got into a disagreement. When this happened, they did not consider the opinion of any one of them to be more valuable. No matter how much experience each one had, his opinion was treated the same as the others. So it took them a long time to reach an agreement. Every time this happened, they had to start from the beginning to reach a solution.

After a while they realized that it would save time, and help their friendship, if they could shorten their disagreements. They decided that it would certainly help if they considered the most valuable opinion first.

Then, if they could agree on that one, they would not have to waste time, and possibly even become less friendly, by arguing about the other two.

Fortunately, they all thought the most valuable opinion was the one based on the most experience. Therefore, they could live together even more peacefully if they gave higher respect to the oldest among them. Only if his opinion were clearly wrong, would they need to consider others.

Unfortunately, the elephant and the monkey and the quail had no idea which one was the oldest. Since this was a time before old age was respected, they had no reason to remember their birthdays or their ages.

Then one day, while they were relaxing in the shade of the big banyan tree, the quail and the monkey asked the elephant, "As far back as you can remember, what was the size of this banyan tree?"

The elephant replied, "I remember this tree for a very long time. When I was just a little baby, I used to scratch my belly by rubbing it over the tender shoots on top of this banyan tree."

Then the monkey said, "When I was a curious baby monkey, I used to sit and examine the little seedling banyan tree. Sometimes I used to bend over and nibble its top tender leaves."

The monkey and the elephant asked the quail, "As far back as you can remember, what was the size of this banyan tree?"

The quail said, "When I was young, I was looking for food in a nearby forest. In that forest, there was a big old banyan tree, which was full of ripe berries. I ate some of those berries, and the next day I was standing right here. This was where I let my droppings fall, and the seeds they contained grew up to be this very tree!"

The monkey and the elephant said, "Aha! Sir quail, you must be the oldest. You deserve our respect and honor. From now on we will pay close attention to your words. Based on your wisdom and experience, advise us when we make mistakes. When there are disagreements, we will give the highest place to your opinion. We ask only that you be honest and just."

The quail replied, "I thank you for your respect, and I promise to always do my best to deserve it."

The Buddha then identified the births, saying:

"The elephant was the Venerable Moggallāna. The monkey was the Venerable Sāriputta. And the wise little quail was I who have become the fully enlightened Buddha."

The moral: "Respect for the wisdom of elders leads to harmony."

38

The Crane and the Crab
[Trickery]
(*Baka-Jātaka*)

There was in Jetavana monastery, a monk who made beautiful robes. He was very much appreciated by all the monks. But, he would give monks old robes that he had repaired, and in exchange they would give him new cloth.

A monk would come to him with new cloth, and request that he make him a robe. He would say that it takes a great deal of time to cut and stitch a new robe, but that he has one already made that the monk can have immediately. So the monk would give him the new cloth and take the old repaired robe. In a few days time, after washing the robe, the monk would understand that he had been tricked.

There was also a robe maker in a nearby village who used to trick people the same way. The monks told him that there was a robe maker in Jetavana who was just like him. So he decided to go to him to get a new robe made. And he put on a beautiful repaired robe that he had made himself.

When he went to the monk, the monk saw his beautiful robe and wanted it for himself. So he gave the village robe maker new cloth to make another robe for himself in exchange for it. But after wearing this robe, and washing it, the monk became aware that he had been deceived himself.

One day, the monks gathered in the preaching hall were discussing this among themselves. When the Buddha entered, he asked them about what they were talking, and they told him. The Buddha said, "Oh monks, not only today, but also in the past this Jetavana robe maker deceived others. And just as he was deceived now by the robe maker from the country, so was he deceived by him in the past."

The monks then asked the Buddha to tell the story of the past. And the Buddha told the past story.

This is how it was:

Once upon a time, there was a crane who lived near a small pond. Right next to the pond was a big tree with a fairy living in it. He learned by observing the various animals.

There were also many small fish living in the small pond. The crane was in the habit of picking up fish with his beak and eating them. Since there happened to be a drought in the area, the water level in the pond was becoming lower and lower. This made it easier for the crane to catch fish. In fact, he was even getting to be a little fat!

However, the crane discovered that no matter how easy it was to catch fish, and no matter how many he ate, he was never completely satisfied. But he did not learn from this. Instead, he decided that if he ate all the fish in the pond, then he would find true happiness. "The more the merrier!" he said to himself.

In order to catch all the fish in the pond, the crane thought up a clever plan. He would trick the fish, and deceive them into trusting him. Then when they trusted him the most, he would gobble them up. He was very pleased with himself for thinking up such a trick.

To begin with, the crane sat down on the shore. He remained quietly in one position, just like a holy man in the forest. This was intended to get the fish to trust him.

The fish came to him and asked, "Sir crane, what are you thinking?" The holy-looking crane answered, "Oh my dear fish, it makes me sad to think of your future. I am thinking about the coming miserable disaster."

They said, "My lord, what disaster is coming to us?" To which the crane replied, "Look around you! There is very little water left in this pond. You are also running out of food to eat. This severe drought is very dangerous for you poor little ones."

Then the fish asked, "Dear uncle crane, what can we do to save ourselves?" "My poor little children," said the crane, "you must trust me and do as I say. If you allow me to pick you up in my beak, I will take you, one at a time, to another pond. That pond is much bigger than this one. It is filled with water and covered with lovely lotuses. It will be like a paradise for you!"

When they heard the part about the beak, the fish became a little suspicious. They said, "Mr. Crane, how can we believe you? Since the beginning of the world, there has never been a crane who wanted to help fish. Cranes have put fish in their beaks only to eat them. This must be a trick. Or else you must be joking!"

The crane then raised his head and made himself look as dignified as possible. He said, "Please don't think such a thing. Can't you see that I am a very special crane? You should trust me. But if you don't believe me, send one fish with me and I will show him the beautiful pond. Then when I bring him back here, you will know I can be trusted."

The fish said to each other, "This crane looks so dignified. He sounds like an honest crane. But just in case it's a trick, let us send with him a useless little troublemaker fish. This will be a test." Then they found a young fish who was known for playing hooky from school. They pushed him towards the shore.

The crane bent his head and picked up the little one in his beak. Then he spread his wings and flew to a big tree on the shore of a beautiful big pond. Just as he had said, it was covered with lovely lotuses. The fish was amazed to see such a wonderful place. Then the crane carried him back to his poor old pond, just as he had promised.

Arriving home, the little fish described the wonders of the beautiful big pond. Hearing this, all the other fish became very excited and rushed to be the first to go.

The first lucky passenger was that same useless little troublemaker. Again the crane picked him up in his beak and flew to the big tree on the shore of the beautiful new pond. The little one was sure the helpful crane was about to drop him into the wonderful pond. But instead, the crane suddenly killed him, gobbled up his flesh, and let the bones fall to the ground.

The crane returned to the old pond, brought the next little fish to the same tree, and ate him in the same way. Likewise, one by one, he gobbled up every last fish!

He became so stuffed with fish meat that he had trouble flying back to the little pond. He saw that there were no more fish left for him to trick and eat. Then he noticed a lonely crab crawling along the muddy shore. And he realized that he was still not completely satisfied!

So he walked over to the crab and said, "My dear crab, I have kindly carried all the fish to a wonderful big pond not far from here. Why do you wish to remain here alone? If you simply do as the fish have done, and let me pick you up in my beak, I will gladly take you there. For your own good, please trust me."

But the crab thought, "There is no doubt this over-stuffed crane has eaten all those fish. His belly is so full he can hardly stand up straight. He definitely cannot be trusted! If I can get him to carry me to a new pond and put me in it, so much the better. But if he tries to eat me, I will have to cut off his head with my sharp claws."

Then the crab said, "My friend crane, I am afraid I am much too heavy for you to carry in your beak. You would surely drop me along the way. Instead, I will grab onto your neck with my eight legs, and then you can safely carry me to my new home."

The crane was so used to playing tricks on others, that he did not imagine he would be in any danger – even though the crab would be grasping him by the throat. Instead he thought, "Excellent! This will give me a chance to eat the sweet meat of this foolish trusting crab."

So the crane permitted the crab to grab onto his neck with all eight legs. In addition, he grasped the crane's neck with his sharp claws. He said, "Now kindly take me to the new pond."

The foolish crane, with his neck in the clutches of the crab, flew to the same big tree next to the new pond.

Then the crab said, "Hey you stupid crane, have you lost your way? You have not taken me to the pond. Why don't you take me to the shore and put me in?"

The crane said, "Who are you calling stupid? I don't have to take that from you. You're not my relative. I suppose you thought you tricked me into giving you a free ride. But I'm the clever one. Just look at all those

fish bones under this tree. I've eaten all the fish, and now I'm going to eat you too, you stupid crab!"

The crab replied, "Those fish were eaten because they were foolish enough to trust you. But no one would trust you now. Because you tricked the fish, you have become so conceited you think you can trick anyone. But you can't fool me. I have you by the throat. So if one dies, we both die!"

Then the crane realized the danger he was in. He begged the crab, "Oh my lord crab, please release me. I have learned my lesson. You can trust me. I have no desire to eat such a handsome crab as you."

Then he flew down to the shore and continued, "Now please release me. For your own good, please trust me."

But this old crab had been around. He realized the crane could not be trusted no matter what he said. He knew that if he let go of the crane, he would be eaten for sure. So he cut through his neck with his claws, just like a knife through butter! And the crane's head fell on the ground. Then the crab crawled safely into the wonderful pond.

Meanwhile, the inquisitive fairy had also come to the new pond and seen all that had happened. Sitting on the very top of the big tree, he said for all the gods to hear:

"The one who lived by tricks and lies,
  No longer trusted now he dies."

The Buddha then ended this Jātaka story by identifying the births:

"The crane was this Jetavana robe maker. The crab was the robe maker from the country. And the fairy who lived in the big tree was I who have become the Buddha."

The moral: "The trickster who can't be trusted has played his last trick."

39

Buried Treasure
[The Arrogance of Power]
(Nanda-Jātaka)

The Buddha told this story while he was living at Jetavana monastery with regard to a disciple of Sāriputta. This monk was very modest in nature. But when he went on an alms pilgrimage to a distant place with the Venerable Sāriputta, he became very proud and arrogant due to the attention he received. The elder Sāriputta mentioned this to the Buddha. And the Buddha said that this monk was also like this in the past. And the Buddha then related this story at the request of the Venerable Sāriputta.

The Buddha said:

Once upon a time, there was an old man who lived in Benares. He had a very good friend, who was known to be wise. Luckily, or perhaps unluckily, he also had a beautiful young wife.

The old man and his young wife had a son. The man came to love his son very much. One day he thought, "I have learned that my beautiful young wife cannot always be trusted. When I die, I am sure she will marry another man, and together they will waste the wealth I have worked so hard for. Later on, there will be nothing left for my son to inherit from his mother. So I will do something to guarantee an inheritance for my deserving son. I will bury my wealth to protect it for him."

Then he called for his most faithful servant, Nanda. Together they took all the old man's wealth deep into the forest and buried it. He said, "My dear Nanda, I know you are obedient and faithful. After I die, you must give this treasure to my son. Keep it a secret until then. When you give the treasure to him, advise him to use it wisely and generously."

Before long, the old man died. Several years later, his son completed his education. He returned home to take his place as the head of the family. His mother said, "My son, being a suspicious man, your father has hidden his wealth. I am sure that his faithful servant, Nanda, knows where it is. You should ask him to show you. Then you can get married and support the whole family."

So the son went to Nanda and asked him if he knew where his father had hidden his wealth. Nanda told him that the treasure was buried in the forest, and that he knew the exact spot.

Then the two of them took a basket and a shovel into the forest. When they arrived at the place the treasure was buried, all of a sudden Nanda became puffed up with how important he was. Although he was only a servant, he had the power of being the only one to know the secret. So he became conceited and thought he was better than the son. He said, "You son of a servant girl! Where would you inherit a treasure from?"

The patient son did not talk back to his father's servant. He suffered his abuse, even though it puzzled him. After a short time, they returned home empty-handed.

This strange behavior was repeated two more times. The son thought, "At home, Nanda appears willing to reveal the secret of the treasure. But when we go into the forest, carrying the basket and shovel, he is no longer willing. I wonder why he changes his mind each time."

He decided to take this puzzle to his father's wise old friend. He went to him and described what had happened.

The wise old man said, "Go again with Nanda into the forest. Watch where he stands when he abuses you, which he surely will do. Then send him away saying, 'You have no right to speak to me that way. Leave me.'

"Dig up the ground on that very spot and you will find your inheritance. Nanda is a weak man. Therefore, when he comes closest to his little bit of power, he turns it into abuse."

The son followed this advice exactly. Sure enough, he found the buried treasure. As his father had hoped, he generously used the wealth for the benefit of many.

The Buddha then identified the births in this way:

"Nanda at that time was this disciple of the Venerable Sāriputta. And the father's wise old friend was I who am today the Buddha."

The moral: "A little power soon goes to the head of one not used to it."

40

The Silent Buddha
[Generosity]
(*Khadiraṅgāra-Jātaka*)

The Buddha told this story while living in Jetavana temple with regard to Anāthapiṇḍika.

The devout merchant Anāthapiṇḍika's house was seven stories high and had seven gateways. Over the fourth gateway there dwelt a deity with her children. Whenever the Buddha would visit, she would have to come down to the ground floor and stay to the side with her head below that of the Buddha on account of the Buddha's splendidity due to his previous meritorious deeds. So also, when various monks in the Buddha's order would come to Anāthapiṇḍika's house for alms and other purposes, she would have to come down to the ground floor because of their merit.

In order to try to put an end to Anāthapiṇḍika's generosity to the Buddha's order, so as to stop the incessant coming and going, she admonished first Anāthapiṇḍika's manager, and then his eldest son, that such munificence could not continue indefinitely without Anāthapiṇḍika becoming bankrupt, but in vain. She dared not approach Anāthapiṇḍika himself.

Eventually, Anāthapiṇḍika did in fact exhaust his wealth. But still he gave the Buddha and his followers whatever fare he could. At that point, the deity felt bold enough to approach him. And she warned him of impending disaster if he did not stop his giving. But he became angry with her, and ordered her and her children out of the house. She had to obey.

In despair, she sought the aid of Sakka, the king of the gods. He suggested that she should recover for the merchant Anāthapiṇḍika all his debts, revealing to him hidden treasure of which he had lost sight. She did so. But Anāthapiṇḍika, before pardoning her, took her to the Buddha.

The Buddha then related this story with regard to Anāthapiṇḍika's firmness in his faith despite this deity's attempts to stop him from giving support to the Buddha.

The Buddha said:

Once upon a time, there was a very rich man living in Benares, in northern India. When his father died, he inherited even more wealth. He thought, "Why should I use this treasure for myself alone? Let my fellow beings also benefit from these riches."

So he built dining halls at the four gates of the city – North, East, South and West. In these halls he gave food freely to all who wished it. He became famous for his generosity. It also became known that he and his followers were practicers of the Five Training Steps [pañca-sīla-s, the first five sikkhā-pada-s].

In those days, there was a Silent Buddha [Pacceka-Buddha] meditating in the forest near Benares.

He was called Buddha because he was enlightened. This means that he no longer experienced himself, the one called 'I' or 'me', as being in any way different from all life living itself. So he was able to experience life as it really is, in every present moment.

Being one with all life, he was filled with compassion and sympathy for the unhappiness of all beings. So he wished to teach and help them to be enlightened just as he was. But the time of our story was a most unfortunate time, a very sad time. It was a time when no one else was able to understand the Truth [Dhamma], and experience life as it really is. And since this Buddha knew this, that was why he was Silent.

While meditating in the forest, the Silent Buddha entered into a very high mental state. His concentration was so great that he remained in one position for seven days and nights, without eating or drinking.

When he returned to the ordinary state, he was in danger of dying from starvation. At the usual time of day, he went to collect alms food at the mansion of the rich man of Benares.

When the rich man had just sat down to have lunch, he saw the Silent Buddha coming with his alms bowl. He rose from his seat respectfully. He told his servant to go and give alms to him.

Meanwhile, Māra, the god of death, had been watching. Māra is the one who is filled with greed for power over all beings. He can only have this power because of the fear of death.

Since a Buddha lives life fully in each moment, he has no desire for future life, and no fear of future death. Therefore, since Māra could have no power over the Silent Buddha, he wished to destroy him. When he saw that he was near death from starvation, he knew that he had a good chance of succeeding.

Before the servant could place the food in the Silent Buddha's alms bowl, Māra caused a deep pit of red-hot burning coals to appear between them. It seemed like the entrance to a hell world.

When he saw this, the servant was frightened to death. He ran back to his master. The rich man asked him why he returned without giving the alms food. He replied, "My lord, there is a deep pit full of red-hot burning coals just in front of the Silent Buddha."

The rich man thought, "This man must be seeing things!" So he sent another servant with alms food. He also was frightened by the same pit of fiery coals. Several servants were sent, but all returned frightened to death.

Then the master thought, "There is no doubt that Māra, the god of death, must be trying to prevent my wholesome deed of giving alms food to the Silent Buddha. Because wholesome deeds are the beginning of the path to enlightenment, this Māra wishes to stop me at all costs. But he does not understand my confidence in the Silent Buddha, and my determination to give."

So he himself took the alms food to the Silent Buddha. He too saw the flames rising from the fiery pit. Then he looked up and saw the terrible god of death, floating above in the sky. He asked, "Who are you?" Māra replied, "I am the god of death!"

"Did you create this pit of fire?" asked the man. "I did," said the god. "Why did you do so?" "To keep you from giving alms food, and in this way to cause the Silent Buddha to die! Also to prevent your wholesome deed from helping you on the path to enlightenment, so you will remain in my power!"

The rich man of Benares said, "Oh, Māra, god of death, the evil one, you cannot kill the Silent Buddha, and you cannot prevent my wholesome giving! Let us see whose determination is stronger!"

Then he looked across the raging pit of fire, and said to the calm and gentle Enlightened One, "Oh Silent Buddha, let the light of Truth continue to shine as an example to us. Accept this gift of life!"

So saying, he forgot himself entirely, and in that moment there was no fear of death. As he stepped into the burning pit, he felt himself being lifted up by a beautiful cool lotus blossom. The pollen from this miraculous flower spread into the air, and covered him with the glowing color of gold. While standing in the heart of the lotus, the Great Being [Bodhisatta] poured the alms food into the bowl of the Silent Buddha. Māra, god of death, was defeated!

In appreciation for this wonderful gift, the Silent Buddha raised his hand in blessing. The rich man bowed in homage, joining his hands above his head. Then the Silent Buddha departed from Benares, and went to the Himalayan forests.

Still standing on the wonderful lotus, glowing with the color of gold, the generous master taught his followers. He told them that practicing the Five Training Steps is necessary to purify the mind. He told them that with such a pure mind, there is great merit in giving alms – indeed it is truly the gift of life!

When he had finished teaching, the fiery pit and the lovely cool lotus completely disappeared.

The Buddha then finalized this Jātaka story, saying:

"The Silent Buddha of those days passed away, never to be born again. And I myself was the very rich man living in Benares who defeated

Māra and, standing on a lotus blossom, poured alms into the bowl of the Silent Buddha."

The moral: "Have no fear when doing wholesome deeds."

The Curse of Mittavinda
(Losaka-Jātaka)

The Buddha told this story while he was dwelling in Jetavana monastery, about the elder Losaka Tissa.

The father of Losaka Tissa was a fisherman of Kosala. In his village, there lived 1,000 families; and on the day he was conceived, no one caught any fish. From that time on, various misfortunes gradually befell them. By a process of exclusion, they discovered that their misfortunes were due to Losaka's family. And, therefore, they drove them out.

As soon as Losaka could walk, his mother put a broken piece of pottery in his hand and sent him out to beg. And she abandoned him.

He wandered about, unkempt and uncared for, picking up lumps of discarded rice, like a crow.

One day, when he was seven years old, the Venerable Sāriputta saw him and, feeling pity for him, ordained him. But he was always unlucky. Wherever he went, begging for alms, he received little and never had a real meal.

In due course, he became a saint [Arahant]. And when the time came for him to die, Sāriputta decided that he should have a proper meal.

He went with Losaka to the populous city of Sāvatthi to beg alms, but no one would even notice them. So he took Losaka back to the monastery and, having collected food himself, sent it back to Losaka. But the messengers with whom he sent it, ate it themselves. When Sāriputta discovered this, it was after noontime. So he went to the king's palace. The king ordered that Sāriputta's bowl be taken and, as it was past noon and no longer time to eat rice or other solid foods, he filled his bowl with honey, ghee, butter, and sugar. Sāriputta took this to Losaka and asked him to eat out of the bowl as Sāriputta held it – in case the food should vanish.

So, the Venerable elder Losaka Tissa ate the sweets, while Sāriputta stood holding the bowl.

That night Losaka died, never to be born again. And a shrine was built to house his collected ashes.

One day, the monks seated in the preaching hall were questioning how it was that the elder Losaka Tissa, though so unlucky, came to win sainthood. When the Buddha entered, he asked, "Oh monks, what were you talking about before I came here?" And the monks told him. "Oh monks," the Buddha said, "Losaka's own actions were the cause both of his receiving so little and of his attaining sainthood. In the past, he prevented others from receiving. And that is why he received so little himself. But it was through his meditation and his meritorious deeds in this life and even in his past, that he won sainthood for himself." And saying this, the Buddha told the story of the past.

This is how it was:

Chapter 1. Jealousy

Once upon a time, there was a monk who lived in a tiny monastery in a little village. He was very fortunate that the village rich man supported him in the monastery. He never had to worry about the cares of the world. His alms food was always provided automatically by the rich man.

So the monk was calm and peaceful in his mind. There was no fear of losing his comfort and his daily food. There was no desire for greater comforts and pleasures of the world. Instead, he was free to practice the correct conduct of a monk, always trying to eliminate his faults and do only wholesome deeds. But he didn't know just how lucky he was!

One day an elder monk arrived in the little village. He had followed the path of Truth [Dhamma] until he had become perfect and faultless.

When the village rich man saw this unknown monk, he was very pleased by his gentle manner and his calm attitude. So he invited him into his home. He gave him food to eat, and he thought himself very fortunate to hear a short teaching from him. He then invited him to take shelter at the village monastery. He said, "I will visit you there this evening, to make sure all is well."

When the perfect monk arrived at the monastery, he met the village monk. They greeted each other pleasantly. Then the village monk asked, "Have you had your lunch today?" The other replied, "Yes, I was given lunch by the supporter of this monastery. He also invited me to take shelter here."

The village monk took him to a room and left him there. The perfect monk passed his time in meditation.

Later that evening, the village rich man came. He brought fruit drinks, flowers and lamp oil, in honor of the visiting holy man. He asked the village monk, "Where is our guest?" He told him what room he had given him.

The man went to the room, bowed respectfully, and greeted the perfect monk. Again he appreciated hearing the way of Truth as taught by the rare faultless one.

Afterwards, as evening approached, he lit the lamps and offered the flowers at the monastery's lovely temple shrine. He invited both monks to lunch at his home the next day. Then he left and returned home.

In the evening, a terrible thing happened. The village monk, who had been so contented, allowed the poison of jealousy to creep into his mind. He thought, "The village rich man has made it easy for me here. He provides shelter each night and fills my belly once a day.

"But I'm afraid this will change because he respects this new monk so highly. If he remains in this monastery, my supporter may stop caring for me. Therefore, I must make sure the new monk does not stay."

Thinking in this way, he lost his former mental calm. His mind became disturbed due to his jealousy – the fear of losing his comfort and his daily food. This led to the added mental pain of resentment against the perfect monk. He began plotting and scheming to get rid of him.

Late that night, as was the custom, the monks met together to end the day. The perfect monk spoke in his usual friendly way, but the village monk would not speak to him at all.

So the wise monk understood that he was jealous and resentful. He thought, "This monk does not understand my freedom from attachment to families, people and comforts. I am free of any desire to remain here. I am also free of any desire to leave here. It makes no difference. It is sad this other one cannot understand nonattachment. I pity him for the price he must pay for his ignorance."

He returned to his room, closed the door, and meditated in a high mental state throughout the night.

The next day, when it was time to go collect alms food from the supporter of the monastery, the village monk rang the temple gong. But he rang it by tapping it lightly with his fingernail. Even the birds in the temple courtyard could not hear the tiny sound.

Then he went to the visiting monk's room and knocked on the door. But again he only tapped lightly with his fingernail. Even the little mice inside the walls could not hear the silent tapping.

Having done his courteous duty in such a tricky way, he went to the rich man's home. The man bowed respectfully to the monk, took his alms bowl, and asked, "Where is the new monk, our visitor?"

The village monk replied, "I have not seen him. I rang the gong, I knocked at his door, but he did not appear. Perhaps he was not used to such rich food as you gave him yesterday. Perhaps he is still asleep, busily digesting it, dreaming of his next feast! Perhaps this is the kind of monk who pleases you so much!"

Meanwhile, back at the monastery, the perfect monk awoke. He cleaned himself and put on his robe. Then he calmly departed to collect alms food wherever he happened to find it.

The rich man fed the village monk the richest of food. It was delicious and sweet, made from rice, milk, butter, sugar and honey. When the monk had eaten his fill, the man took his bowl, scrubbed it clean, and sweetened it with perfumed water. He filled it up again with the same wonderful food. He gave it back to the monk, saying, "Honorable monk, our holy visitor must be worn out from traveling. Please take my humble alms food to him." Saying nothing, he accepted the generous gift for the other.

By now the village monk's mind was trapped by its own jealous scheming. He thought, "If that other monk eats this fantastic meal, even if I grabbed him by the throat and kicked him out, he still would never leave! I must secretly get rid of this alms food. But if I give it to a stranger, it will become known and talked about. If I throw it away in a pond, the butter will float on the surface and be discovered. If I throw it away on the ground, crows will come from miles around to feast on it, and that too would be noticed. So how can I get rid of it?"

Then he saw a field that had just been burned by farmers to enrich the soil. It was covered with hot glowing coals. So he threw the rich man's generous gift on the coals. The alms food burned up without a trace. And with it went his peace of mind!

For when he got back to the monastery, he found the visitor gone. He thought, "This must have been a perfectly wise monk. He must have known I was jealous – afraid of losing my favored position. He must have known I resented him and tried to trick him into leaving. I wasted alms food meant for him. And all for the sake of keeping my own belly full! I'm afraid something terrible will happen to me! What have I done?" So, afraid of losing his easy daily food, he had thrown away his peace of mind.

For the rest of his life the rich man continued to support him. But his mind was filled with torment and suffering. He felt doomed like a walking starving zombie, or a living hungry ghost.

When he died, his torment continued. For he was reborn in a hell world, where he suffered for hundreds of thousands of years.

Finally, there too he died, as all beings must. But the results of his past actions were only partly completed. So he was reborn as a demon, 500 times! In those 500 lives, there was only one day when he got enough to eat, and that was a meal of afterbirth dropped by a deer in the forest!

Then he was reborn as a starving stray dog – another 500 times! For the sake of a full monk's belly in a past life, all these 500 lives were also filled with hunger, and quarreling over food. Only a single time did he get enough to eat, and that was a meal of vomit he found in a gutter!

Finally most of the results of his actions were finished. Only then was he so very fortunate enough to be reborn as a human being. He was born into the poorest of the poor beggar families of the city of Kāsi, in northern India. He was given the name, Mittavinda.

From the moment of his birth, this poor family became even more poor and miserable. After a few years, the pain of hunger became so great, that his parents beat him and chased Mittavinda away for good. They shouted, "Be gone forever! You are nothing but a curse!"

Poor Mittavinda! So very long ago he had not known how lucky he was. He was contented as a humble village monk. But he allowed the poison of jealousy to enter his mind – the fear of losing his easy daily food. This led to the self-torture of resentment against a perfect monk, and to trickery in denying him one wholesome gift of alms food. And it took a thousand and one lives for the loss of his comfort and daily food to be completed. What he had feared, his own actions had brought to pass!

Chapter 2. Greed

Little did poor Mittavinda know that his lives of constant hunger were about to come to an end. After wandering about, he eventually ended up in Benares.

At that time the Enlightenment Being was living the life of a world-famous teacher in Benares. He had 500 students. As an act of charity, the people of the city supported these poor students with food. They also paid the teacher's fees for teaching them.

Mittavinda was permitted to join them. He began studying under the great teacher. And at last, he began eating regularly.

But he paid no attention to the teachings of the wise master. He was disobedient and violent. During 500 lives as a hungry dog, quarreling had become a habit. So he constantly got into fist fights with the other students.

It became so bad that many of the students quit. The income of the world-famous teacher dwindled down to almost nothing. Because of all his fighting, Mittavinda was finally forced to run away from Benares.

He found his way to a small remote village. He lived there as a hard-working laborer, married a very poor woman, and had two children.

It became known that he had studied under the world-famous teacher of Benares. So the poor villagers selected him to give advice when questions arose. They provided a place for him to live near the entrance to the village. And they began following his advice.

But things did not go well. The village was fined seven times by the king. Seven times their houses were burned. And seven times the town pond dried up.

They realized that all their troubles began when they started taking Mittavinda's advice. So they chased him and his family out of the village. They shouted, "Be gone forever! You are nothing but a curse!"

While they were fleeing, they went through a haunted forest. Demons came out of the shadows and killed and ate his wife and children. But Mittavinda escaped.

He made his way to a seaport city. He was lonely, miserable and penniless. It just so happened that there was a kind generous rich merchant living in the city. He heard the story of Mittavinda's misfortunes. Since they had no children of their own, he and his wife adopted Mittavinda. For better or worse they treated him exactly as their own son.

His new mother and father were very religious. They always tried to do wholesome things. But Mittavinda still had not learned his lesson. He did not accept any religion, so he often did unwholesome things.

Some time after his father's death, his mother decided to try and help him enter the religious life. She said, "There is this world and there is the one to come. If you do bad things, you will suffer painful results in both worlds."

But foolish Mittavinda replied, "I will do whatever I enjoy doing and become happier and happier. There is no point considering whether what I do is wholesome or unwholesome. I don't care about such things!"

On the next full moon holy day, Mittavinda's mother advised him to go to the temple and listen all night long to the wise words of the monks. He said, "I wouldn't waste my time!" So she said, "When you return I will give you a thousand gold coins."

Mittavinda thought that with enough money he could enjoy himself constantly and be happy all the time. So he went to the temple. But he sat in a corner, paid no attention, and fell asleep for the night. Early the next morning he went home to collect his reward.

Meanwhile his mother thought he would appreciate wise teachings. Then he would bring the oldest monk home with him. So she prepared delicious food for the expected guest. When she saw him returning alone, she said, "Oh my son, why didn't you ask the senior monk to come home with you for breakfast?"

He said, "I did not go to the temple to listen to a monk or to bring him home with me. I went only to get your thousand gold coins!" His disappointed mother said, "Never mind the money. Since there is so much delicious food prepared – only eat and sleep!" He replied, "Until you give me the money, I refuse to eat!" So she gave him the thousand gold coins. Only then did he gobble up the food until all he could do was fall asleep.

Mittavinda did not think a thousand gold coins were enough for him to constantly enjoy himself. So he used the money to start a business, and before long he became very rich. One day he came home and said, "Mother, I now have 120,000 gold coins. But I am not yet satisfied. Therefore I will go abroad on the next ship and make even more money!"

She replied, "Oh my son, why do you want to go abroad? The ocean is dangerous and it is very risky doing business in a strange land. I have 80,000 gold coins right here in the house. That is enough for you. Please don't go, my only son!"

Then she held him to keep him from leaving. But Mittavinda was crazy with greed. So he pushed his mother's hand away and slapped her face. She fell to the floor. She was so hurt and shocked that she yelled at him, "Be gone forever! You are nothing but a curse!"

Without looking back, Mittavinda rushed to the harbor and set sail on the first departing ship.

Chapter 3. Pleasure

After seven days on the Indian Ocean, all the winds and currents stopped completely. The ship was stuck! After being dead in the water for seven days, all on board were terrified they would die.

So they drew straws to find out who was the cause of their bad luck and frightening misfortune. Seven times the short straw was drawn by Mittavinda!

They forced him onto a tiny bamboo raft, and set him adrift on the open seas. They shouted, "Be gone forever! You are nothing but a curse!" And suddenly a strong wind sent the ship on its way.

But once again Mittavinda's life was spared. This was a result of his wholesome actions as a monk, so many births ago. No matter how long it takes, actions cause results.

Sometimes an action causes more than one result, some pleasant and some unpleasant. It is said there are Asura-s who live through such mixed results in an unusual way.

Asura-s are unfortunate ugly gods. Some of them are lucky enough to change their form into beautiful young dancing girl goddesses. These are called Apsaras-es.

They enjoy the greatest pleasures for seven days. But then they must go to a hell world and suffer torments as hungry ghosts for seven days. Again they become Apsaras goddesses – back and forth, back and forth – until both kinds of results are finished.

While floating on the tiny bamboo raft, it just so happened that Mittavinda came to a lovely Glass Palace. There he met four very pretty Apsaras-es. They enjoyed their time together, filled with heavenly pleasures, for seven days.

Then, when it was time for the goddesses to become hungry ghosts, they said to Mittavinda, "Wait for us just seven short days, and we will return and continue our pleasure."

The Glass Palace and the four Apsaras-es disappeared. But still Mittavinda had not regained the peace of mind thrown away by the village monk, so very long ago. Seven days of pleasure had not satisfied him. He could not wait for the lovely goddesses to return. He wanted more and more. So he continued on, in the little bamboo raft.

Lo and behold, he came to a shining Silver Palace, with eight Apsaras goddesses living there. Again he enjoyed seven days of the greatest pleasure. These Apsaras-es also asked him to wait the next seven days, and disappeared into a hell world.

Amazing as it may seem, the greedy Mittavinda went on to seven days of pleasure in a sparkling Jewel Palace with 16 Apsaras-es. But they too disappeared. Then he spent seven days in a glowing Golden Palace with 32 of the most beautiful Apsaras-es of all.

But still he was not satisfied! When all 32 asked him to wait seven days, again he departed on the raft.

Before long he came to the entrance of a hell world filled with suffering tortured beings. They were living through the results of their own actions. But his desire for more pleasure was so strong that Mittavinda thought he saw a beautiful city surrounded by a wall with four fabulous gates. He thought, "I will go inside and make myself king!"

After he entered, he saw one of the victims of this hell world. He had a collar around his neck that spun like a wheel, with five sharp blades cutting into his face, head, chest and back. But Mittavinda was still so greedy for pleasure that he could not see the pain right before his eyes. Instead he saw the spinning collar of cutting blades as if it were a lovely lotus blossom. He saw the dripping blood as if it were the red powder of perfumed sandalwood. And the screams of pain from the poor victim sounded like the sweetest of songs!

He said to the poor man, "You've had that lovely lotus crown long enough! Give it to me, for I deserve to wear it now." The condemned man warned him, "This is a cutting collar, a wheel of blades." But Mittavinda said, "You only say that because you don't want to give it up."

The victim thought, "At last the results of my past unwholesome deeds must be completed. Like me, this poor fool must be here for striking his mother. I will give him the wheel of pain." So he said, "Since you want it so badly, take the lotus crown!"

With these words the wheel of blades spun off the former victim's neck and began spinning around the head of Mittavinda. And suddenly all his illusions disappeared – he knew this was no beautiful city, but a terrible hell world; he knew this was no lotus crown, but a cutting wheel of blades; and he knew he was not king, but prisoner. Groaning in pain he cried out desperately, "Take back your wheel! Take back your wheel!" But the other one had disappeared.

Just then the king of the gods arrived for a teaching visit to the hell world. Mittavinda asked him, "Oh king of gods, what have I done to deserve this torment?" The god replied, "Refusing to listen to the words of monks, you obtained no wisdom, but only money. A thousand gold coins did not satisfy you, nor even 120,000. Blinded by greed, you struck your mother on your way to grabbing greater wealth still.

"Then the pleasure of four Apsaras-es in their Glass Palace did not satisfy you. Neither eight Apsaras-es in a Silver Palace, nor 16 in a Jewel Palace. Not even the pleasure of 32 lovely goddesses in a Golden Palace was enough for you! Blinded by greed for pleasure you wished to be king. Now at last, you see your crown is only a wheel of torture, and your kingdom is a hell world.

"Learn this, Mittavinda – all who follow their greed wherever it leads are left unsatisfied. For it is in the nature of greed to be dissatisfied with what one has, whether a little or a lot. The more obtained, the more desired – until the circle of greed becomes the circle of pain."

Having said this, the god returned to his heaven world home. At the same time the wheel crashed down on Mittavinda. With his head spinning in pain, he found himself adrift on the tiny bamboo raft.

Soon he came to an island inhabited by a powerful she-devil. She happened to be disguised as a goat. Being hungry, Mittavinda thought nothing of grabbing the goat by a hind leg. And the she-devil hiding inside kicked him way up into the air. He finally landed in a thorn bush on the outskirts of Benares!

After he untangled himself from the thorns, he saw some goats grazing nearby. He wanted very badly to return to the palaces and the dancing girl Apsaras-es. Remembering that a goat had kicked him here, he grabbed the leg of one of these goats. He hoped it would kick him back to the island.

Instead, this goat only cried out. The shepherds came, and captured Mittavinda for trying to steal one of the king's goats.

As he was being taken as a prisoner to the king, they passed by the world-famous teacher of Benares. Immediately he recognized his student. He asked the shepherds, "Where are you taking this man?"

They said, "He is a goat thief! We are taking him to the king for punishment!" The teacher said, "Please don't do so. He is one of my students. Release him to me, so he can be a servant in my school." They agreed and left him there.

The teacher asked Mittavinda, "What has happened to you since you left me?"

He told the story of being first respected, and then cursed, by the people of the remote village. He told of getting married and having two children, only to see them killed and eaten by demons in the haunted forest. He told of slapping his generous mother when he was crazy with greed for money. He told of being cursed by his shipmates and being cast adrift on a bamboo raft. He told of the four palaces with their beautiful goddesses, and how each time his pleasure ended he was left unsatisfied. He told of the cutting wheel of torture, the reward for the greedy in hell. And he told of his hunger for goat meat, that only got him kicked back to Benares without even a bite to eat!

The world-famous teacher said, "It is clear that your past actions have caused both unpleasant and pleasant results, and that both are eventually completed. But you cannot understand that pleasures always come to an end. Instead, you let them feed your greed for more and more. You are left exhausted and unsatisfied, madly grasping at goat legs! Calm down, my friend. And know that trying to hold water in a tight fist, will always leave you thirsty!"

Hearing this, Mittavinda bowed respectfully to the great teacher. He begged to be allowed to follow him as a student. The Enlightenment Being welcomed him with open arms.

* * *

The Buddha said:

"This elder Losaka Tissa was himself the cause both of his getting little and of his obtaining sainthood.

"The elder Losaka Tissa was Mittavinda in former days. And I who have become the Buddha was in the past the world-famous teacher."

The moral: "In peace of mind, there is neither loss nor gain."

The Pigeon and the Crow
[The Danger of Greed]
(*Kapota-Jātaka*)

The Buddha told this story while dwelling at Jetavana temple about a greedy monk. The story of its narration will be told in the ninth book in the *Kāka-Jātaka*.[22]

The Buddha, having heard of this monk's greed, summoned him. While he was among the assembled monks, the Buddha said, "It is not good to be greedy." And without invitation, he told this story of the past:

Once upon a time, the people of Benares were fond of setting up birdhouses. This was an act of generosity and kindness, done for the comfort of birds. It also made the people happy to hear the friendly birds singing.

The richest man in the city had a cook. He kept such a birdhouse near the kitchen. In it lived a gentle and careful pigeon. He was so gentle that he did not care to eat meat. And he was careful to keep his distance from the cook. For he knew the cook was in the habit of roasting and boiling dead animals, even including birds!

So the pigeon always left the birdhouse early in the morning. After spending the day finding and eating his food, he returned each night to sleep in the birdhouse. He was quite contented with his calm and harmless life.

Nearby there was a crow who was quite a different sort of character. For one thing, he would eat anything! And he was not known for being gentle and careful. Instead, he often became overly excited, and acted

---

22 There is no *Kāka-Jātaka* in the ninth book, however.

without considering the danger. And far from being contented, he often got himself into trouble.

One day the crow smelled the delicious food being cooked in the rich man's kitchen. He was so attracted by the odor that he could not take his mind off it. He decided that he must have the rich man's meat at any cost. So he began spying on the kitchen, trying to figure out a way to get some of the meat and fish.

As usual, that evening the pigeon returned with his little belly satisfied, and contentedly entered his little home for the night. Seeing this, the hungry crow thought, "Ah, wonderful! I can make use of this dull pigeon to grab a delicious feast from the kitchen."

The next morning, the crow followed the pigeon when he left for the day. The pigeon asked him, "Oh my friend, why are you following me?" The crow replied, "Sir, I like you very much, and I admire your calm and regular way of life. From now on, I would like to assist you and learn from you."

The pigeon said, "Friend crow, your life style is much more exciting than mine. You would get bored following me around. And you don't even eat the same food I do. So how can you assist me?"

The crow said, "When you go each day to find your food, we will separate and I will find my food. In the evening, we will come back together. Being together, we will be able to help and protect each other." The pigeon said, "That sounds all right to me. Now go your own way and work hard finding food."

The pigeon spent his usual day eating grass seeds. It took some time patiently searching for a few little grass seeds, but he was satisfied and contented.

The crow spent the day turning over cow dung patties, so he could gobble up the worms and insects he found there. This was fairly easy work, but he kept thinking it would be even easier to steal from the rich man's kitchen. And no doubt the food would be better too!

When he was full, he went to the pigeon and said, "Sir pigeon, you spend too much time searching for and eating food. It is no good wasting

the whole day that way. Let us go home." But the pigeon kept on steadily eating grass seeds, one by one. He was quite happy that way.

At the end of the day, the impatient crow followed the pigeon back to his birdhouse. They slept in it together peacefully. They spent several days and nights in this way.

Then one day there was a delivery of many kinds of fresh meat and fish. The cook hung them on hooks in the kitchen for storage.

The crow saw this and was overwhelmed by the sight of so much food. His desire became greed, and he began plotting a way to get it all for himself. He decided to pretend to be sick. So he spent the entire night groaning and moaning.

The next morning, the pigeon was ready to go look for food as usual. The crow said, "Go without me, sir pigeon, I have been sick to my stomach all night long."

The pigeon replied, "My dear crow, that sounds so strange. I've never heard of a crow getting an upset stomach. But I have heard they sometimes faint from hunger. I suspect you want to gobble up as much as you can of the meat and fish in the kitchen. But it's for people, not crows. People don't eat pigeon food. Pigeons don't eat crow food. And it would not be wise for you to eat people food. It might even be dangerous! So come with me as usual, and be satisfied with crow food, sir crow!"

The crow said, "I'm too sick, friend pigeon, I'm too sick. Go ahead without me."

"Very well," said the pigeon, "but your actions will speak louder than your words. I warn you, don't risk safety for the sake of greed. Be patient until I return." Then the pigeon left for the day.

But the crow paid no attention. He thought only about grabbing a big piece of fish, and was glad to be rid of the pigeon. "Let him eat grass seeds!" he thought.

Meanwhile, the cook prepared the meat and fish in a big stew pot. While it was cooking, he kept the lid slightly off, to allow the steam to escape. The crow smelled the delicious fragrance in the rising steam. Watching from the birdhouse, he saw the cook go outside to rest from the heat.

The crow saw that this was the chance he'd been waiting for. So he flew into the kitchen and sat on the edge of the stew pot. First he looked for the biggest piece of fish he could find. Then he stuck his head inside and reached for it. But in so doing, he knocked the lid off! The clattering sound brought the cook into the kitchen at once.

He saw the crow standing on the edge of the pot – with a fish bigger than he was, hanging from his beak! Immediately, he closed the door and window of the kitchen. He thought, "This food is for the rich man. I work for him, not for some mangy crow! I will teach him a lesson he'll never forget!"

The poor crow could not have picked a worse enemy. This cook just happened to be rather ignorant, so he did not mind being cruel when he had the upper hand. He took no pity at all on the clever crow.

He grabbed him, and plucked out all his feathers. The poor crow looked ridiculous without his shining black feathers. Then the vengeful cook made a spicy paste from ginger, salt and chili peppers. He rubbed it all over the crow's pink sore skin. Then he put him on the floor of the birdhouse, and laughed.

The crow sweated and suffered from the terrible burning pain. He cried in agony all day long.

In the evening, the pigeon returned from a quiet day searching for and eating grass seeds. He was shocked to see the terrible state of his friend the crow. He said, "Obviously, you didn't listen to me at all. Your greed has done you in. I'm so sad there's nothing I can do to save you. And I'm afraid to stay in this birdhouse so close to that cruel cook. I must leave at once!"

So the careful pigeon flew away in search of a safer birdhouse. And the plucked and pasted crow died a painful death.

"The crow was this monk today. And the pigeon was I who have become the Buddha."

The moral: "Greed makes one deaf to sound advice."

43

Bamboo's Father
[Wasted Advice]
(Veḷuka-Jātaka)

The Buddha told this story while waiting at Jetavana temple about a monk who did not pay attention to his elders' words. The Buddha asked this monk, "Is it true that you do not pay attention to your elders' words?" The Buddha then said, "Not only today, but even in the past, by not listening to elders' advice you came to ruin." And the Buddha told a story of the past:

Once upon a time, there was a teacher who meditated much and developed his mind. Gradually his fame spread. Those who wished to be guided by a wise man came to hear him. Considering what he said to be wise indeed, 500 decided to become his followers.

One of these 500, who considered his teachings to be wise, was a certain pet lover. In fact, he loved pets so much that there was no animal he did not wish to keep as a pet.

One day he came upon a cute little poisonous snake, who was searching for food. He decided he would make an excellent pet. So he made a little bamboo cage to keep him in when he had to leave him alone. The other followers called the little snake, 'Bamboo' [Veḷuka]. Because he was so fond of his pet, they called the pet lover, 'Bamboo's Father' [Veḷuka-pitā].

Before long, the teacher heard that one of his followers was keeping a poisonous snake as a pet. He called him to him and asked if this was true. Bamboo's Father said, "Yes master, I love him like my own child!"

The wise teacher said, "It is not safe to live with a poisonous snake. Therefore, I advise you to let him go, for your own good."

But Bamboo's Father thought he knew better. He replied, "This little one is my son. He wouldn't bite me. I can't give him up and live all alone!"

The teacher warned him, "Then surely, this little one will be the death of you!" But the follower did not heed his master's warning.

Later on, all 500 of the teacher's followers went on a trip to collect fresh fruits. Bamboo's Father left his 'son' locked up in the bamboo cage.

Since there were many fruits to collect, it was several days before they returned. Bamboo's Father realized that poor Bamboo had not eaten the whole time he was away. So he opened the cage to let him out to find food.

But when he reached inside, his 'son' bit his hand. Having been neglected for all that time, Bamboo was angry as well as hungry. Since he was only a snake, he didn't know anything about poison!

But his 'father' should have known better. After all, he had been warned by the very teacher he himself considered wise.

Within minutes of being bitten, Bamboo's Father dropped dead!

The Buddha said:

"Bamboo's Father in those days was this monk today. And the teacher was I who have become the Buddha."

The moral: "There's no benefit in following a teacher if you don't listen to what he says."

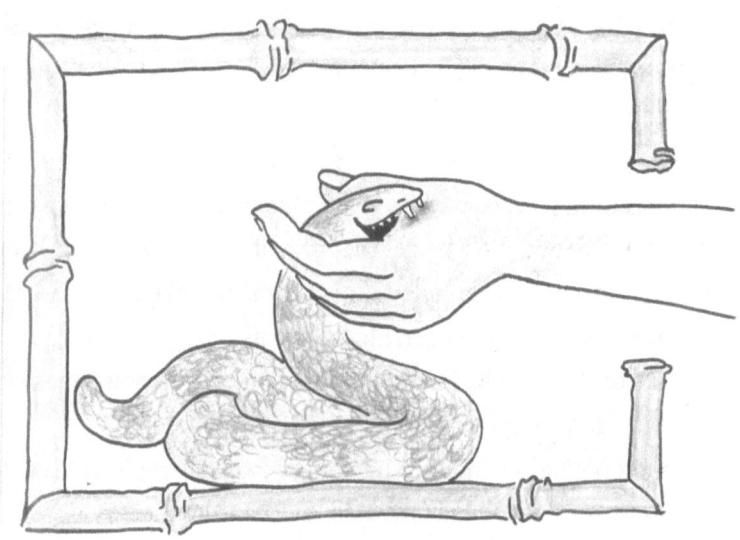

Two Stupid Children
[Foolishness]
(Makasa-Jātaka)

The Buddha told this story while on pilgrimage in Magadha.

In a certain village in Magadha there dwelt a lot of foolish people who were vexed by mosquitoes when working in the jungle. One day, they armed themselves with bows and arrows and went into the jungle to shoot the mosquitoes, but instead just shot and struck one another.

When the Buddha came to this village, he saw all the injured men and asked what had happened. When told, he said, "This is not the first time you foolish people have done this. Even in your past lives, there were those who trying to kill a mosquito, hit a fellow creature instead." And the Buddha told this story of the past:

* * *

(Rohiṇī-Jātaka)

The Buddha told this story while dwelling at Jetavana monastery about a servant girl of the millionaire Anāthapiṇḍika named Rohiṇī.

One day, when the girl was pounding rice, her mother lay down near her and flies settled on her and stung her. When she asked her daughter to drive them away, her daughter lifted her pestle and hit her with it, thinking to kill the flies. But instead of the flies, she killed her mother.

This news was told to the Buddha by Anāthapiṇḍika. The Buddha said to Anāthapiṇḍika, "This girl did the very same thing in past times, too." And invited by Anāthapiṇḍika, the Buddha told this story:

* * *

Once upon a time, there was an old carpenter with a shiny bald head. On sunny days, his head shined so brightly that people shaded their eyes when talking to him!

On just such a sunny day, a hungry mosquito was attracted to the old carpenter's bright bald head. He landed on it and started biting into it.

The carpenter was busy smoothing a piece of wood with a plane. When he felt the mosquito biting him, he tried to chase him away. But the hungry mosquito would not leave such a good-looking meal. So the man called over his son and asked him to get rid of the stubborn pest.

Unlike his father's shiny head, the son was not so bright. But he was hard-working and obedient. He said, "Don't worry Dad, be patient. I'll kill that bug with just one blow!"

Then he picked up a very sharp ax, and took careful aim at the mosquito. Without thinking, he came down with the ax and split the mosquito in two! Unfortunately, after slicing through the mosquito, the

Meanwhile, an adviser to the king happened to be passing by with his followers. They saw what had just happened, and were quite shocked that anyone could be so stupid!

The king's adviser said, "Don't be so surprised by human stupidity! This reminds me of a similar event that occurred just yesterday.

"In a village not far from here, a woman was cleaning rice. She was pounding it in a mortar with a pestle, to separate the husks. As she worked up a sweat, a swarm of flies began buzzing around her head. She tried to chase them away, but the thirsty flies would not leave.

"Then she called over her daughter [Rohiṇī] and asked her to shoo away the bothersome bugs. Although she was a rather foolish girl, the daughter always tried her best to please her mother.

"So she stood up from her own mortar, raised her pestle, and took careful aim at the biggest and boldest of the flies. Without thinking, she pounded the fly to death! But of course, the same blow that killed the fly, also ended her mother's life.

"You all know what they say," said the adviser, finishing his story, "'With friends like these, who needs enemies!'"

* * *

44. The Buddha then said:

"The king's adviser was I who am today the Buddha."

* * *

45. The story told, the Buddha identified the births in this way:

"The mother and daughter in the past were the same as the mother and daughter today."

The moral: "A wise enemy is less dangerous than a foolish friend."

Watering the Garden
[Foolishness]
(Ārāmadūsaka-Jātaka)

The Buddha told this story while visiting a village in Kosala on alms round.

A rich householder in the village invited the Buddha and his followers to lunch. After lunch, he told them they could walk around his garden. While some of the monks were walking around it, they saw a bare area. They asked the gardener why this area was bare. The gardener said that it was caused by a lad who had been asked to water the plants there, but who before watering them, pulled them out to see the size of their roots so as to know how much water to give them.

The monks reported this story to the Buddha. The Buddha said, "This is not the first time that village lad has spoiled a garden. He did the very same in past times, too." And saying this, the Buddha told this story of the past:

It was just before New Year's in Benares, in northern India. Everyone in the city was getting ready for the three-day celebration, including the gardener of the king's pleasure garden.

There was a large troop of monkeys living in this pleasure garden. So they wouldn't have to think too much, they always followed the advice of their leader, the monkey king.

The royal gardener wanted to celebrate the New Year's holiday, just like everybody else. So he decided to hand over his duties to the monkeys.

He went to the monkey king and said, "Oh king of monkeys, my honorable friend, would you do a little favor for me? New Year's is coming.

I too wish to celebrate. So I must be away for three full days. Here in this lovely garden, there are plenty of fruits and berries and nuts to eat. You and your subjects may be my guests, and eat as much as you wish. In return, please water the young trees and plants while I'm gone."

The monkey king replied, "Don't worry about a thing, my friend! We will do a terrific job! Have a good time!"

The gardener showed the monkeys where the watering buckets were kept. Feeling confident, he left to celebrate the holiday. The monkeys called after him, "Happy New Year!"

The next day, the monkeys filled up the buckets, and began watering the young trees and plants. Then the king of the monkeys addressed them: "My subjects, it is not good to waste water. Therefore, pull up each young tree or plant before watering. Inspect it to see how long the roots are. Then give more water to the ones with long roots, and less water to the ones with short roots. That way we will not waste water, and the gardener will be pleased!"

Without giving it any further thought, the obedient subjects followed their king's orders.

Meanwhile, a wise man was walking by outside the entrance to the garden. He saw the monkeys uprooting all the lovely young trees and plants, measuring their roots, and carefully pouring water into the holes in the ground. He asked, "Oh foolish monkeys, what do you think you're doing to the king's beautiful garden?"

They answered, "We are watering the trees and plants, without wasting water! We were commanded to do so by our lord king."

The man said, "If this is the wisdom of the wisest among you – the king – what are the rest of you like? Intending to do a worthwhile deed, your foolishness turns it into disaster!"

The Buddha then identified the births:

"The monkey king in those times was this village lad. And the wise man was I who have become the Buddha."

The moral: "Only fools can make good deeds into bad ones."

47

Salty Liquor [Foolishness]
(*Vāruṇi-Jātaka*)

The Buddha told this story while dwelling in Jetavana monastery about someone who spoiled good liquor.

The millionaire Anāthapiṇḍika had a friend who was a tavern owner. The tavern owner prepared a batch of strong liquor that he intended to sell for cash only. He then left his bartender in charge while he went to bathe in a nearby river. The bartender saw that after the customers drank the liquor, they ate a little salt. He thought that the liquor needed salt to taste good, so he added salt to the liquor. No sooner did the customers taste this, than they spit it out. Crying out that he had spoiled the liquor, they abused him. And one after another, they left the tavern. When the tavern owner returned, he did not see a single customer. He asked the bartender where they had all gone, and the bartender told him what had happened. The tavern owner reprimanded him, and went off and told Anāthapiṇḍika. Anāthapiṇḍika, thinking that this was a good story to tell, went to Jetavana temple where he told the Buddha about it.

The Buddha said, "This is not the first time this man has spoiled liquor. He did just the same thing before." Then, at Anāthapiṇḍika's asking, the Buddha told this story of the past:

Once upon a time, there was a tavern owner in Benares. He had a hard-working bartender [Koṇḍañña], who was always trying to be helpful by inventing new ways of doing things.

One hot day, the tavern owner wanted to bathe in a nearby river. So he left the bartender in charge while he was gone.

The bartender had always wondered why most of the customers ate a little salt after drinking their liquor. Not wishing to show his ignorance, he never bothered to ask them why they did this. He did not know that they ate the salt in order to chase away the aftertaste of the liquor. He thought it needed salt to taste good.

He wondered why taverns did not add salt to their liquor. He decided that if he did so, the business would make much higher profits, and the tavern owner would be very pleased. So he added salt to all the liquor!

To his surprise, when the customers came to the tavern and drank the salty liquor, they immediately spit it out and went to a different bar.

When the owner returned from his dip in the river, he found his tavern without customers, and all his liquor ruined.

So he went and told this story to his friend, an adviser to the king. The adviser said, "The ignorant, wishing only to do good, often cannot help doing harm."

The Buddha said:

"The bartender in the past is the same as the bartender today. And the king's adviser was I who am today the Buddha."

The moral: "The best intentions are no excuse for ignorance."

48

The Magic Priest and the Kidnaper Gang
[Power and Greed]
(Vedabbha-Jātaka)

The Buddha told this story while he was dwelling in Jetavana temple about a monk who did not like to pay attention to others' advice. The Buddha said to him, "Because you did not listen to the advice of the wise in the past also, you came to ruin." And saying this, the Buddha told the story of the past:

Once upon a time in Benares, there was a king named Brahmadatta. In one of the kingdom's remote villages, there was a priest who had magical power. He knew a special magic spell, which was a secret given to him by his teacher.

This spell could be used only once a year, when the planets were lined up in a certain way. Only then, the priest could say the secret magic words into his open palms. Then he looked up into the sky, clapped his hands, and a shower of precious jewels came down on him.

The magic priest was also a teacher. He had a very good student who was intelligent and able to understand the most difficult ideas. He was obedient and faithful, always wishing to honor and protect his master.

One day, the priest had to go on a trip to a faraway village in order to perform an animal sacrifice. Since he had to take a dangerous road, the good student went with him.

Along this road there happened to be a gang of 500 bandits. They were known as the 'Kidnaper Gang' [Gahaṇa Kula]. They captured people and demanded ransom money in return for letting them live.

Lo and behold, the magic priest and his good student were captured by the Kidnaper Gang. They set the ransom at 5,000 gold coins, and sent the student to go get it, in order to save his master's life.

Before leaving, the student knelt before his teacher and bowed respectfully. He said to him quietly, so the bandits could not hear, "Oh master, tonight is the one night of the year when the planets will be lined up perfectly. Only then can your magic spell be used to shower you with jewels from the sky. However, I must warn you, my beloved and respected teacher, that to use such a power to save yourself from such greedy men as these, would be extremely dangerous. Obtaining great wealth so easily must lead to disaster for men like them. And if you think only of your own safety, bringing such harm to them will cause danger to you as well.

"Therefore, I warn you, do not give in to the desire to make the spell of jewels. Let the lucky night pass by for this year. Even if these bandits harm you, trust your faithful student to save you, without adding to your danger." So saying, he took his leave.

That evening, the kidnapers tied up the magic priest tightly, and left him outside their cave for the night. They gave him nothing to eat or drink.

After the moon came out, the priest saw the planets lining up so his spell could work. He thought, "Why should I suffer like this? I can magically pay my own ransom. Why should I care if harm comes to these 500 kidnapers? I am a magic priest. My life is worth much more than theirs. I care only for my own life. And besides, this lucky night only comes but once a year. I cannot waste the chance to use my great power!"

Having decided to ignore the advice of the good student, he called the kidnapers and said, "Oh brave and mighty ones, why do you want to tie me up and make me suffer?"

They replied, "Oh holy priest, we need money. We have many mouths to feed. We must have money, and lots of it!"

The magic priest said, "Ah, you did this for money? Is that all there is to it? In that case, I will make you rich beyond your wildest dreams! For I am great and powerful. As a holy priest, you can trust me. You must untie me, wash my head and face, dress me in new clothes, and cover me with flowers. Then, after so honoring me properly, leave me alone to do my magic."

The kidnapers followed his instructions. But, not trusting him completely, they hid in the bushes and secretly watched him.

This is what they saw. The washed and flower-covered priest looked up into the sky. Seeing that the planets were lined up in the special lucky pattern, he lowered his head and muttered the magic spell into his hands. They were sounds that no one could understand, something like this: "*Nah Wah Shed-nath. Eel Neeah Med-rak. Goh Bah Mil-neeay.*"

Then he gazed into the sky and clapped his hands. Suddenly he was showered with the most beautiful jewels!

The Kidnaper Gang came out from hiding and grabbed all the precious stones. They wrapped them up in bundles and went off down the road, with the magic priest following behind.

On the way, they were stopped by another gang of 500 robbers. They asked them, "Why are you stopping us?" "Give us all your wealth!" the others demanded.

The kidnapers said, "Leave us alone. You can get all the riches you want from this magic priest, just as we have done. He says magic words, looks up into the sky, claps his hands, and the most fabulous jewels come down!"

So they let the Kidnaper Gang go, and surrounded the priest. They demanded that he make a shower of precious stones for them as well.

He said, "Of course I can give you all the jewels you want. But you must be patient and wait for one year. The lucky time, when the planets are lined up properly, has already come this year. It will not happen again until next year. Come see me then, and I will be happy to make you rich!"

Robbers are not exactly known for their patience. They became angry at once. They shouted at him, "Ah, you tricky lying priest! You made the Kidnaper Gang wealthy, but now you refuse to do the same for us. We'll teach you to take us so lightly!" Then they cut him in two with a sharp sword, and left both halves of his body in the middle of the road.

The robbers chased after the Kidnaper Gang. There was a terrible bloody battle. After hours of fighting, they killed all 500 kidnapers and stole the wonderful jewels.

As soon as they left the battleground, the 500 robbers began quarreling over the wealth. They divided into two rival groups of 250 each. These fought another bloody battle, until only two were left alive, one from each side.

These two collected all the valuable jewels and hid them in the forest. They were very hungry. So one guarded the treasure, while the other started cooking rice.

The one doing the guarding thought, "When the other is finished cooking, I will kill him and keep all this loot for myself!"

Meanwhile, the one doing the cooking thought, "If we divide these jewels in two, I will get less. Therefore, I will add poison to this rice, kill the other, and keep all the jewels for myself. Why share, when I can have it all!"

So he ate some of the rice, since he was so hungry, and poisoned the rest. He took the rice pot to the other and offered it to him. But he immediately swung his sword and chopped off the cook's head!

Then the hungry killer began gobbling up the poisoned rice. Within minutes, he dropped dead on the spot!

A few days later, the good student returned with the ransom money. He could not find his teacher or the Kidnaper Gang. Instead, he found only the worthless possessions they had left behind after getting the jewels.

Continuing down the road, he came to the two halves of his teacher's dead body. Realizing that the magic priest must have ignored his warning, he mourned his cruel death. Then he built a funeral pyre, covered it with wildflowers, and burned the body of his respected teacher.

A little farther down the road, the good student came upon the 500 dead bodies of the Kidnaper Gang. Farther still, he started seeing the dead robbers, until he counted 498.

Then he saw the footprints of the last two going into the forest. He realized that they too must fight over the treasure, so he followed them. Finally, he came to the dead body slumped over the rice pot, the other one with his head chopped off, and the bundles of valuable jewels. He could tell immediately what had happened.

He thought, "It is so sad. My teacher had great knowledge, but not enough common sense. He could not resist using his magical power, regardless of the results. By causing the deaths of the one thousand greedy gangsters, he doomed himself as well."

The good student took the treasure back to the village, and used it generously for the benefit of many.

The Buddha said:

"The magic priest in the past was this self-willed monk today. And his student was I who have today become the Buddha."

The moral: "When power has no conscience, and greed has no limit – the killing has no end."

49

The Groom Who Lost His Bride to the Stars
[Astrology]
(Nakkhatta-Jātaka)

The Buddha told this story with regard to two families of Sāvatthi, one of which lived in the nearby countryside, and a certain naked ascetic.

The family living in the countryside set a day for their son's wedding. But only afterward, they went to consult a naked ascetic with whom the family was familiar with regard to whether or not the day would be auspicious. The ascetic, angry that he had not been consulted in the first place, decided to obstruct the wedding. He told them that the day was unlucky. The family then decided to postpone the wedding.

On the day of the wedding, when the groom did not arrive, the bride's family gave their daughter to another groom.

The following day, at the advice of the naked ascetic who said that the stars, planets and moon were now in auspicious positions, the groom and his family came to claim the bride. And the bride's family said, "We have given the maiden to another groom. You picked the date, and then we spent a lot of money in the preparations. But you disgraced us, and did not come. So we gave the girl to someone else."

A quarrel followed. But in the end, the country family went home the way they came.

One day, the monks in the preaching hall were discussing how this naked ascetic had disrupted the marriage. When the Buddha entered, he asked, "Oh monks, what were you talking about before I came here?" The monks told him, and the Buddha said, "Oh monks, this is not the first time this ascetic has disrupted the marriage ceremony of that family. Out of anger, he did just the same thing before." And the Buddha told this story of the past:

Once upon a time, there was a rich family living in Benares, in northern India. They arranged for their son to marry a good and honest girl from a nearby village. Being very pretty as well, they were sure they could not find a better wife for their son.

The groom's family decided on a date for the wedding. The bride's family agreed to meet them in the village on the wedding day.

Meanwhile, the rich family also had their own special astrological priest. When he found out they had picked the wedding day, without paying him to consult the stars, he became angry. He decided to get even with them.

When the wedding day arrived, the astrological priest dressed up in his finest robes, and called the family together. He bowed to them all, and then looked at his star charts very seriously. He told them that this star was too close to the horizon, and that planet was in the middle of an unlucky constellation, and the moon was in a very dangerous phase for having a wedding. He told them that, not seeking his advice, they had picked the worst day of the year for a wedding. This could only lead to a terrible marriage.

The frightened family forgot all about the wonderful qualities of the intended bride, and remained home in Benares.

Meanwhile, the bride's family had arranged everything for the village wedding ceremony. When the agreed upon hour arrived, they waited and waited for the future husband and his family. Finally they realized they were not coming. So they thought, "Those city people picked the date and time, and now they didn't show up. This is insulting! Why should we wait any longer? Let our daughter marry an honorable and hard-working village man." So they quickly arranged a new marriage and celebrated the wedding.

The next day, the astrological priest said that, suddenly, the stars and planets and moon were in perfect positions for a wedding! So the

Benares family went to the village and asked for the wedding to take place. But the village people said, "You picked the date and time. Then you disgraced us by not showing up!"

The city people replied, "Our family priest told us that yesterday the stars and planets and moon were in terrible positions. It was a very unlucky day for a wedding. But he has assured us that today is a most lucky day. So please send us the bride at once!"

The village family said, "You have no honor. You have made the choice of the day more important than the choice of the bride. It's too late now! Our daughter has married another." Then the two families began to quarrel heatedly.

A wise man happened to come along. Seeing the two families quarreling so, he tried to settle the dispute.

The city people told him that they had respected the warnings of their astrological priest. It was because of the unlucky positions of the stars and planets and moon, that they had not come to the wedding.

The wise man said, "The good fortune was in the bride, not in the stars. You fools have followed the stars and lost the bride. Without your foolishness, those far-off stars can do nothing!"

After telling this Jātaka story, the Buddha connected the births in this way:

"The ascetic today is the same as the astrological priest of the past, and both families are also the same. And I who have become the Buddha was the wise man who happened to come along."

The moral: "Luck comes from actions, not from stars."

50

The Prince Who Had a Plan
[The Power of Superstition]
(Dummedha-Jātaka)

The Buddha told this story while he was dwelling in Jetavana monastery with regard to preventing unwise actions that are done for the general good. The story with regard to its narration will be told in the twelfth book in the *Mahākaṇha-Jātaka* [No. 469].

[This story was told with regard to the Buddha's altruism.

One day, in the evening when the Buddha was sitting in the preaching hall, he asked the monks what they were talking about before he entered. The monks told him that they were talking about his walking on foot so as to preach to the five monks who had practiced asceticism together with him before he attained enlightenment,[23] to King Mahākappina,[24] and also for the benefit of the demon Āḷavaka,[25] and many others. Such was his exemplary service for the benefit of others.

When the Buddha heard such praise from the monks for his exemplary actions, he said, "Oh monks, such deeds were done by me also in the past." Then the monks requested that he disclose one of the several stories of his altruistic deeds in the past. And the Buddha told a story.]

Once upon a time, King Brahmadatta was ruling in Benares, in northern India. The Enlightenment Being was born as his son, the prince.

---

23 The Pañcavaggiyā Bhikkhu-s, the five monks who accompanied the Buddha when he began to practice asceticism, are Koṇḍañña, Bhaddiya, Vappa, Mahānāma, and Assajji.

24 King Mahākappina was a wealthy king who became one of the Buddha's most eminent disciples.

25 The conversion of the demon Āḷavaka is considered to be one of the chief incidents of the Buddha's life.

Being quite intelligent, he completed his entire education by the age of 16. So, at this early age, his father made him second in command.

In those days, most people in Benares worshipped gods. They were very superstitious. They thought gods caused things to happen to them, rather than being results of their own actions. So they would pray to these gods and ask special favors. They would ask for a lucky marriage, or the birth of a child, or riches, or fame.

They would promise the gods that, if their prayers were answered, they would pay them by making offerings to them. In addition to flowers and perfumes, they imagined the gods desired the sacrifice of animals. So, when they thought the gods had helped them, they killed many animals – goats, lambs, chickens, pigs and others.

The prince saw all this and thought, "These helpless animals are also subjects of the king, so I must protect them. The people commit these unwholesome acts due to ignorance and superstition. This cannot be true religion. For true religion offers life as it really is, not killing. True religion offers peace of mind, not cruelty.

"I fear these people believe in their superstitions too strongly to give them up. This is very sad. But perhaps their beliefs can at least be put to good use. Someday I will become king. So I must begin to make a plan to let their superstitions help them. If they must offer sacrifices, let them kill their own greed and hatred, instead of these helpless animals! Then the whole kingdom will benefit."

So the prince devised a clever long-term plan. Every so often, he rode in his grand chariot to a popular banyan tree just outside the city. This was a huge tree, where the people prayed and made offerings to a god they thought lived there. The prince came down from his chariot and made the same offerings as the others – incense, flowers, perfumes and water – but *not* animal sacrifices.

In this way he made a great show, and the news spread about his offerings. Pretty soon, all the people thought he was a true believer in the great god of the banyan tree.

In due time, King Brahmadatta died and his son became king. He ruled as a righteous king, and the people benefited. So all his subjects came to trust and respect him as a just and honorable king.

Then one day, he decided it was the right time to carry out the rest of his plan. So he called all the leading citizens of Benares to the royal assembly hall. He asked them, "Worthy ministers and loyal subjects, do you know how I was able to make sure that I would become king?" No one could answer.

He said, "Do you remember that I often gave wonderful sweet offerings to the great god of the banyan tree?" "Yes, our lord," they said.

The king continued, "At each of those times, I made a promise to the powerful god of the tree. I prayed, 'Oh mighty one, if you make me King of Benares, I will offer a special sacrifice to you, far greater than flowers and perfumes.'

"Since I am now the king, you all can see for yourselves that the god has answered my prayers. So now I must keep my promise and offer the special sacrifice."

All those in the assembly hall agreed. They said, "We must prepare this sacrifice at once. What animals do you wish to kill?"

The king said, "My dear subjects, I am glad you are so willing to cooperate. I promised the great god of the banyan tree that I would sacrifice anyone who fails to practice the Five Training Steps [*pañca-sīla-s*, the first five *sikkhā-pada-s*]. That is, anyone who destroys life, takes what is not given, does wrong in sexual ways, speaks falsely, or loses his mind from alcohol. I promised that, if any do these things, I will offer their guts, and their flesh and blood on the great god's altar!"

Being so superstitious, all those in the hall agreed that this must be done, or the god would surely punish the king and the kingdom.

The king thought, "Ah, such is the power of superstition that these people have lost all common sense! They cannot see that, since the first training step is to give up killing, if I sacrificed one of my subjects, I would be next on the altar! And such is the power of superstition that I could make such a promise, and never have to carry it out!"

So, with full confidence in the power of superstition, the king said to the leading citizens, "Go into all the kingdom and announce the promise I made to the god. Then proclaim that the first one thousand who break any of the training steps will have the honor of being sacrificed, to keep the king's promise."

Lo and behold, the people of Benares became famous for carefully practicing the Five Training Steps. And the good king, who knew his subjects so well, sacrificed no one.

The Buddha said:

"The ministers and loyal subjects of the righteous king of those days, are the Buddha's disciples today. And the prince who became that righteous king was I who am today the Buddha."

The moral: "Sacrifice your own wrong-doing, not some helpless animal."

Appendix A

Who Was the Bodhisatta?

Some who tell these stories say that they are about past lives of the Buddha, the Enlightened One. Before he became enlightened as the Buddha, he was called the Bodhisatta, the Enlightenment Being. Look at the list below to see who is said to be the Bodhisatta in each story.

1. The wise merchant
2. The tradesman
3. The honest salesman
4. The king's wise adviser
5. The honest price maker
6. Prince Goodspeaker
7. Little Prince No-father
8. The best teacher
9. The king with one gray hair
10. The wise old master
11. The wise old deer
12. King Banyan Deer
13. The wise fairy
14. The King of Benares
15. A wise and respected teacher
16. A wise and respected teacher
17. A gentle forest monk
18. A fairy who lived in a nearby tree
19. The spirit living in the banyan tree
20. The monkey king

21.   The careful antelope

22.   The Dog King Silver

23, 24. The great horse Knowing-one

25.   An intelligent minister who was known for his understanding of animals

26.   An intelligent minister who was known for his understanding of animals

27.   An intelligent minister who was known for his understanding of animals

28.   The bull called Delightful

29.   Grandma's Blackie

30.   Big Red

31.   King Sakka who in his previous life was Magha the Good

32.   King Golden Swan

33.   Quail King

34.   A very wise adviser who understood the speech of animals

35.   The baby quail who could not fly away

36.   The wise old leader

37.   A quail

38.   The inquisitive fairy

39.   The father's wise old friend

40.   The rich man of Benares

41.   The world-famous teacher

42.   A gentle and careful pigeon

43.   A teacher who meditated much

44, 45. An adviser to the king

46.   A wise man

47.   An adviser to the king

48.   The good student

49.   A wise man

50.   The prince who had a plan

Appendix B

An Arrangement of Morals

The morals from the stories are arranged below, according to three pairs of unwholesome and wholesome qualities. These are: greed and generosity, anger and loving-kindness, delusion and wisdom. This can be used as a different order for reading the stories.

Moral	Story	Page
Greed and Generosity		
"It is better to eat to live, than to live to eat."	14	63
Greed makes one deaf to sound advice.	42	178
When power has no conscience, and greed has no limit – the killing has no end.	48	193
In peace of mind, there is neither loss nor gain.	41	165
Anger and Loving-kindness		
There is safety in unity, and danger in conflict.	33	136
Prejudice leads to injustice. Wisdom leads to justice.	22	89
Loving-kindness makes the poorest house into the richest home.	29	116
Even 'natural enemies' can become 'best friends'.	27	108
Weather comes and weather goes, but friendship remains.	17	73
One should always help one's relatives	22	89

Moral	Story	Page
Delusion and Wisdom		

Moral	Story	Page
A fool in high office can bring shame even to a king.	5	19
The trickster who can't be trusted has played his last trick.	38	151
One must always be wise enough not to be fooled by tricky talk and false appearances.	1	1
Don't envy the well-off, until you know the price they pay.	30	120
Infatuation leads to destruction.	13	59
Fools are trapped by their own desires.	34	140
Only fools can make good deeds into bad ones.	46	188
A wise enemy is less dangerous than a foolish friend.	44, 45	185
A little power soon goes to the head of one not used to it.	39	157
If you let pride go to your head, you'll wind up acting like a fool.	32	133
The best intentions are no excuse for ignorance.	47	191
Even animals value cleanliness.	25	101
As rough talk infects with violence, so do gentle words heal with harmlessness.	26	104
Harsh words bring no reward. Respectful words bring honor to all.	28	112
Respect for the wisdom of elders leads to harmony.	37	148
Nothing can be learned from a teacher by one who misses the class.	15	67
There's no benefit in following a teacher if you don't listen to what he says.	43	183
Those who ignore the advice of the wise do so at their own risk.	36	146

Moral	Story	Page
Wherever it is found, compassion is a sign of greatness.	12	51
Truth, wholesomeness and compassion can save the world.	35	143

ABOUT PARIYATTI

Pariyatti is dedicated to providing affordable access to authentic teachings of the Buddha about the Dhamma theory (*pariyatti*) and practice (*paṭipatti*) of Vipassana meditation. A 501(c)(3) non-profit charitable organization since 2002, Pariyatti is sustained by contributions from individuals who appreciate and want to share the incalculable value of the Dhamma teachings. We invite you to visit www.pariyatti.org to learn about our programs, services, and ways to support publishing and other undertakings.

Pariyatti Publishing Imprints

Vipassana Research Publications (focus on Vipassana as taught by S.N. Goenka in the tradition of Sayagyi U Ba Khin)

BPS Pariyatti Editions (selected titles from the Buddhist Publication Society, copublished by Pariyatti)

MPA Pariyatti Editions (selected titles from the Myanmar Pitaka Association, copublished by Pariyatti)

Pariyatti Digital Editions (audio and video titles, including discourses)

Pariyatti Press (classic titles returned to print and inspirational writing by contemporary authors)

Pariyatti enriches the world by

- disseminating the words of the Buddha,
- providing sustenance for the seeker's journey,
- illuminating the meditator's path.

www.ingramcontent.com/pod-product-compliance
Lightning Source LLC
Chambersburg PA
CBHW050514260626
47157CB00004B/1325